Something by Which to Remember Me

Adam J Wolstenholme

ISBN   #:   978-0-244-31769-0

Content ID: 21124143

Contents

The Present

The last time we ever stayed at Harbour Cottage, we woke one morning to find that our holiday had become unrecognisable. I think I was six and you'll have been nearly eight. I remember I still took My Little Pony to bed with me, and you were getting too old for your Transformers. The previous night, Mum and Dad had been drinking and laughing with Uncle Pete and Aunt Clara. We could hear them downstairs as we lay talking in bed. But in the morning it was strangely quiet. We crept downstairs to find bottles, glasses, and abandoned meals scattered around the kitchen. There was broken glass on the floor. Then we heard voices upstairs. Mum shouting and crying, Dad's voice softer, nervously pleading. There was no sound from Pete and Clara's room.

Eventually Dad appeared. His eyes were swollen, red-tinged smudges in his pale face.

"Where are Uncle Pete and Aunt Clara?" you asked. "What's wrong with Mummy?"

Dad looked out of the window at the space where their car had been. "I suppose they had to go. Come on, kids. Let's clear up before Mummy comes down."

When Mum came down she looked even worse than Dad. She was shaking furiously as she bundled us, breakfastless, into our coats and shoes.

"Where are we going?" said Dad.

"*We're* going out," Mum said. "You do what you want. Go find Clara. I'm sure Pete will understand."

Dad just watched as Mum dragged us out of the house and to the car.

She parked at that nearby rocky beach. It was a bright, cold day, still early, and the beach was empty. I took a bucket from the car, but couldn't find a spade and didn't dare to ask for one. In silence we walked down to the old jetty. Suddenly Mum sank down onto the stones and lit a cigarette, shielding it from the wind with a shaking hand.

"Why have you started smoking again?" you said.

"I don't know, Tom. Ask your dad." Mum looked out to sea where a solitary gull was taking dives at something hiding in the shark-grey water.

"Where have Uncle Pete and Aunt Clara gone?" I said.

Mum just looked at me as if she was in pain. I wanted to comfort her, but was afraid I'd done something wrong, she looked so angry. So I just stood there, cold and wretched on the stony beach, clutching my useless bucket.

"Tom, why don't you take your sister for a paddle or something? I'll be along in a minute."

We walked up the beach.

"Let's hide and maybe she'll come looking for

us," you said.

So we climbed over the jetty, out of sight. Eventually we gave up hope of her following and sat, helpless on the stones.

"Tom, why's Mummy so upset?"

"I don't know."

But I felt you knew more than I did, that you and the adult world were keeping from me some vital information upon which my survival might depend.

"Did Mummy fall out with Aunt Clara?" I asked.

You shrugged, gazed off towards the jetty. I thought I saw a thin cloud from Mum's cigarette rise from behind the jetty only to be snatched away in the wind.

I felt we had to *do* something, and began picking up stones and putting them in the bucket. "Let's make Mummy a present."

I was worried that you'd laugh, dismiss the idea as

childish or girlish. But you didn't. You held the bucket while I chose the stones. Sometimes I had to delve down to where they were wet and sandy to find the best ones. I remember feeling reassured with each clink of stone against stone, as if the fullness of the bucket was a defence against our suddenly unpredictable world.

Then you had another idea. You took out the prettiest four stones, packed the bucket almost to the brim with smaller ones, and then placed the four chosen ones on top.

"There we are," you said. "A family of four. Just like ours."

There was nothing else to be done. We clutched the present between us as we made the fearful journey across the stony beach, towards our mother, towards whatever was going to happen next to our family.

Something by which to Remember Me

"You realise this is a test?"

I pushed my Fender Twin further into the van, closed the doors and turned to face her. She stood in the driveway in jeans and bare feet, the tough-girl smile not quite masking the fear in her eyes.

"Then let's pass it," I said.

We embraced and kissed in the way we still did then. Her tears ran into our mouths and we kept on kissing until my phone bleeped – another hurry-up message from our manager, Bob.

"Go on. Give em hell." She swiped at the tears, annoyed with herself. "Break a leg. Whatever."

I looked over my shoulder as I backed out of the driveway – it was barely wide enough for the van - yes, I should have trimmed that hedge - and by the time I straightened up and faced the house again, Amanda had disappeared inside it, invisible behind the small-ish front window that reflected the mid-summer sun.

The house, our first, we bought with the help of a loan from Amanda's dad. They don't give good mortgage deals to musicians, apparently. Not even those featured in the Best Newcomer category of the *NME* awards.

But an hour later I was on the way to London, to the first show of our first UK tour, with two close buddies who knew what it meant to be the *NME's* Best Newcomer. Bob cranked up our single, *The Sweetest Pain.* He gave an un-ironic whoop, opened the windows to let in the breeze and fuck me if it didn't feel like rock n roll.

The *NME* thing didn't impress our mortgage adviser – my generation, prematurely plump and middle-aged in her bank-issue skirt and blouse.

She read the article, shook her head and said, "It's still 'musician', so ..."

"So the computer says no."

"I'm afraid it does."

Amanda gave me an apologetic cringe. Taking the *NME* into the bank had been her idea. I folded the magazine and stuffed it into my bag while Amanda slipped outside to call her dad. The mortgage adviser gazed at her screen, clicking her mouse, and said. "Oh, well. When you're rich and famous I'll be able to say ..."

As if I was in a band to be rich and famous. As if I'd fail if it didn't make me rich and famous. Which I guess I probably would. Because it probably wouldn't. Have you ever said that 'rich and famous' thing to someone in a band? Well, don't. Even if you end up a mortgage adviser.

Our *NME* award *did* impress some girls – girls who read the *NME*, a species now extinct, no doubt, but in those days very much warmly alive. They began hanging around after shows. Bob – newly married, fifty, fatherly in his faded denim and Guns N Roses T-shirt, let us stand around flirting while he packed the bulk of the gear. The girls asked what we were doing now, and usually we were driving on for the next tour date. But sometimes we were staying in a nearby hotel and they wanted to come with us: Test time. It helped that Jake had a girlfriend as well. It helped that our tight budget meant that most nights Jake and I had to share a twin room, and *that* wouldn't work. ("What do you think we are," we liked to say to each other, "Fucking *footballers*?") It helped that most of our fans were teenagers – and I don't have a thing for teenagers. It helped that I loved Amanda.

"But where are all the lads?" I asked as we drove north through the night.

"What do you want lads for?" Jake opened the window, letting in a spattering of rain, and blew smoke out of it. We were drinking the last of the beers from our rider while our kit shifted and clanked in the back. Bob, driving without music so we could rest our ears after the show, hummed our tunes and chewed Nicorette.

"Male fans tend to buy more music," I said. "Girl fans are fickle."

"And where's your evidence for that?"

"Just an instinct."

Maybe I was thinking of Amanda, the scratched, boxless *Best Of* CDs languishing in her glove compartment. (I once told her that Alan Partridge gag. You know the one? Asked his opinion on the best Beatles album, Alan solemnly intones: "I think it would have to be ... *The Best of the Beatles*." Amanda laughed, but did she really get it?)

"Maybe there are more girl fans because we're so damn gorgeous," Jake said.

Meaning they fancied *him*. A fact about Jake: He was very good-looking in those days. And, credit due, he was a great performer. When you picture us on stage, picture him at the front, pushing us out there at the crowd, while I'm the jerk-off further back – strumming the Telecaster, keeping all the electronic shit going with five different pedals. I'd written most of our songs, a fact on which of course Jake preferred not to dwell. Our biggest hit, a mushy ballad, *The Sweetest Pain*, (Did I mention it?) was all mine. It's the sort of song girls like, which probably explained their predominance in our fan base. I didn't remind Jake of this. It was my job to be the mature one.

"They fancy *you*," I said. You see? Gracious.

"That one in the specs seemed more keen on you, mate."

"She was lovely, actually."

"Mmm. Shame we had to leave. Shame you can't do anything anyway since you're shacked up with Amanda."

"It's not a shame," I said, reaching for my phone so I could send her the reassuring post-show text.

I met Amanda in the Starbucks above Borders in our final year at university. I collected my espresso and was looking for a free table when I saw this blonde girl with deep brown eyes and a pleasantly chunky body. I like women who are cool with being alone in public. It bodes well for their self-confidence. I hovered until she caught my eye.

"Mind if I join you?"

"Pleasure," she said, and her lips parted, revealing endearingly crooked teeth. Pleasure …

We were both Lit students and we bonded over books. Her tastes bordered uncomfortably on the stuff

my mum read for her book group. No doubt mine –
Roth, Updike, the big Americans – seemed a bit macho.
But there was enough crossover for us to find common
ground. And how much do you really want in common
anyway? We also bonded over the stuff we both *didn't*
like. When we wandered into the shop, Amanda pointed
at *To Kill a Mockingbird* and said, "What an over-rated
pile of tosh *that* is." I felt emboldened to jerk a derisive
thumb at a film poster of *Breakfast at Tiffany's.* "That's
worse."

Over our second coffee, I mentioned the band.

"No, I haven't heard of you," she said. "But then
I'm hopelessly uncool when it comes to music."

She sounded proud of herself.

So we barely talked about music over that first
summer. Most of it was spent in the attic bedroom of the
house she shared. Then, when the girl who lived in the
room next door began to get a bit catty about the noise
we were making, we switched to my flat for a while. I
lived alone at the time. The night of her first visit, I
made an effort - the session with the bleach and the
toilet brush; the cooking of a meal from my sister's

recipe book, which involved a measuring jug and an aubergine. Then Amanda arrived. She looked great in a snug pair of jeans and a top that stopped above her pierced navel. (The early Noughties was the age of the exposed midriff. Remember that?) She saw the rows of vinyl, the vintage posters, my KORG home studio, the Fender and the Martin.

"Shit, you *do* play in a band, don't you?"

I put on our demo, tried not to mind when, during the second song she got up and began browsing the books on my shelf, actually taking some of them down and reading bits just when it got to the middle-eight that I was so proud of. I tried not to mind because I felt entirely relaxed in her company. Easy, was the word that came to mind. You know that Bryan Adams line about it being so damn easy making love to you? What I love is that the line was probably very easy to write. And it can happen that way. The juices flow. The gold streams out of your pen and you're fucking Amanda like it's an addiction and you can't remember how you ever got through a day without her. You feel a tenderness you didn't know you were capable of. And after a run of

19

difficult girls I was happy to savour an easy one. And she said she didn't want kids, which at the very least kicked *that* whole issue into the long grass, which was where it belonged as far as I was concerned. So what if she wasn't much of a music lover? Insight One: Not giving a shit about music does not necessarily make you a bad person. Insight Two: Giving a shit does not make you a good one. The Nazis and Wagner, remember.

She drove us out for a weekend in the Chilterns, and I was good about not sneering at her *Now That's What I Call Music* CDs. I took my own compilations. I imposed a system of taking turns of three tracks each. She half-listened to my explanations of the songs – Bruce, Cohen, the Beatles, the Stones – and the stories behind them. Then, on the Sunday, driving back, when it was her turn, she said, "I think I'll just have silence for a bit."

"Silence. Okay."

After a moment she said, "Not like, *actual* silence. Talk to me."

And we talked a lot, in a state of fearless liberation. About ourselves, our histories, our exes. But

20

she was also thrillingly knowledgeable. She'd explain stuff – the way the chalk in the Chilterns was formed, how hedge funds worked, the significance of the shadow-cabinet reshuffle, you name it. I just gave up trying to talk about music. But that did mean, for instance, that a song would come on the radio, and it would occur to me to say something about it, and I'd stop myself. That can be a habit that spreads, I find, until you over-think and you lose a certain spontaneity. You're still playing together, but you're not, like, *shredding*.

It became less easy when we bought the house. I worried that the mortgage would … stifle my creativity. Steal my muse. Okay, laugh. The commitment brought with it the spectre of what my mum would have called a 'real job'. Amanda did teacher training and landed what she told me was a plumb job with a sixth form college. Over the long holidays she did a lot of tutoring. So we managed, with the help of her dad who was – and this helped too – something of a bedroom guitarist. (Cherry-red Strat, Straights, Rea).

Amanda would probably say I didn't take enough of an interest in decorating the place. As if I could feel excited about spending an afternoon sanding a door when I should have been in the rehearsal studio with Jake. But no-one could say I didn't put the hours in.

Sex tailed off a bit, big surprise. And it was happening more often that I'd be recognised by some babe when we went out together. So I can see why she thought the first tour was a test. But I was confident of passing it, because I loved her, didn't do drugs or stupid amounts of drinking, which is more than could be said for Jake.

It didn't take *him* long to fail the test. After the Newcastle gig I came back from loading my amp into the van to find Jake snorting a line off the table in what passed for our dressing room. With him was a distressingly attractive gothy-looking girl. You know the type: pale, plump curves straining against leather and metal, exciting those parts of you that you're not especially proud of.

"I'm going back to Jenna's," he declared.

22

"You're bloody not!" Bob had come in behind me and looked furious. It will have been the coke more than anything. Bob had seen his fair share of casualties and wasn't about to preside over another. "We've to be up at seven tomorrow. I'm not taking the risk."

But Jake had coke fizzing in his head and was starting to feel invincible. "*I'm* taking the risk, mate. I'm going back to Jenna's. It's a hall of residence in town. I can meet you in –"

"Bring her with us," I said quickly. "I'll sleep in Bob's room."

And so I spent a night on the floor, listening to Bob snoring and farting, trying not to hear the orgasmic moaning and rattling bed frame through the thin wall, telling myself I'd done a good thing.

In the morning I was woken by the alarm, made instant coffee – the UHT milk, the too-small kettle with its too-short flex – and knocked on Jake's door. Jenna opened it. She was wearing a hotel bath robe, which she let fall open as she reached out and took both mugs. Before turning away, she caught me giving her the once-over and we locked eyes. She stuck out her tongue – in

23

and out, swift as a snake. I still remember that tongue, which was long and plump, and on which a silver stud insolently glittered.

I tolerated Jake moaning about his hangover and bragging about the girl until he sobered up and went sullen. But I drew the line at letting him stretch out across the seats in the van. *I* did that while he morosely chewed gum as we crossed the border under a grey sky.

Something changed at the Glasgow show. I'd worried that Jake would be under-par after his sex-and-drugs session, but he really pulled it out that night. There were girls and boys in the front rows shouting the songs back at us. He reached out, gripped hands and was pulled into the crowd. I watched him consumed as if by a hungry sea and then spat out, shirtless, clambering back on stage. In the spotlight, I could see that female fingernails had scored tracks across his back. You'd be impressed by how well I concealed my jealousy, how maturely I kept this in perspective. The show got a five-star review in *Melody Maker*. On the way to Aberdeen, we got the news that the single had reached number nine. Officially Top Ten! In celebration we upgraded that night so I had a room of my own. I was running a bath when Bob knocked on the door with a champagne miniature and the news that we'd been offered a slot on *Later with Jools Holland.*

Amanda was impressed at last. Her dad had seen the *Melody Maker* piece and called her. When I pulled up in the van she came out of the house to greet me. There was an unmistakable shine of pride in her eyes.

"You *do* play in a band, don't you -?"

We kissed in a way that should have told her everything she needed to know. But still she checked: "So did you pass the test?"

"Of course I did."

We were in the bedroom and she was sitting across me, pulling her top over her head when I remembered to ask, "Did *you* pass?"

What was I hoping for? A coquettish wouldn't-you-like-to-know? smile followed by a discreet affirmative? I didn't quite get that. Amanda laughed, putting something bitterly self-deprecating and not very sexy into it. She balled up her top and chucked it at the wash basket. "Yes I did," she said. "Not that it was much of a test."

***

After the encouraging performance of our first album the label decided it was time to attempt a US tour. Bob didn't put it any more optimistically than that. We weren't going to 'conquer' or 'crack' America. (Remember Suede? Their singer, Brett Anderson used to make enjoyably over-the-top statements in interviews. Asked if he thought Suede could make it in the states, he said America would be 'brought to heel'. Sometimes I thought I lacked the chutzpah to be a proper rock star). But there were signs that America might warm to us. The new folk scene was going by then. Jake had been less resistant than usual to my attempts to take us in a more acousticy direction. He'd have died of shame if he'd known there was anything remotely country going on, but that's where I was taking us. Bob booked us a run down the Eastern seaboard, then the delta blues belt. Jake was annoyingly divided about this. Of course he was wildly excited about the possibilities of a successful American tour. But Bush had just won his second term, which gave Jake all the more confidence in his long-held, unexamined prejudices: Americans were all fat, ignorant, warmongering thugs. Of course I didn't see it that way, with my grounding in Philip Roth, Updike, not to mention -

"- We're talking about the people who invented rock and roll here," I reminded him.

"Yeah, right. And then there's that famous American band, the Beatles."

"Okay, but you know what Lennon said? He'd felt American ever since he heard *Heartbreak Hotel.*"

That shut him up, for a bit.

Amanda was also conflicted. She was convinced by then that I was actually capable of making some money, and she wasn't above enjoying the kudos of living with 'rock star', though she couldn't quite let go of those inverted commas. But then she said -

"- You realise you couldn't do this if we had kids, don't you?"

The taxi was booked. I was doing the last-minute rummage to check passport, boarding pass, plectrums.

"Sorry. I don't know why I said that. Do you really need that coat? It'll be a drag at the airport."

What she said came as such a left-field blow that I didn't know where to start. (What's this about kids? Who *says* I couldn't do it with kids? Are you saying I should quit? If I do, what the fuck else am I supposed to do? I thought you didn't want kids. YOU SAID YOU DIDN'T WANT KIDS!) But her method was becoming familiar, this shoot-and-scoot tactic of making a point without giving me a chance to respond. It was fear, looking back, that was behind it. She was afraid of a discussion because of all the unfaceable shit it would throw up at us once we started digging in those dark corners.

My taxi beeped.

"You could come with us next time," I said, kissing her cheek. "You could play tambourine. The kid could shake a rattle."

Not great, I admit, but what would you have said?

It started well. I loved New York. That feeling of having been there before, in a dream, a sense of returning to a spiritual home. The dream was of course the movies, but also the novels and the music. And Jake's anti-Americanism didn't extend to our female American fans. He was single now, and enjoying himself, though there was a certain urgency about it, like a man downing his penultimate pint so he could get another in before last orders. Did he feel under time pressure because he was losing his hair? It's not the sort of thing you can ask. He let himself down in Pittsburgh. Nothing major, just a bit slurred and clumsy and generally below par. You could feel the crowd notice.

By then I'd been feeling an anxiety of my own. Staring out of the window at the hills of Kentucky, I managed to untangle the issues in my head. There were two of them, possibly related. One: Amanda wanted me to stay at home and have children with her. Two: I hadn't written a song for nearly six months and the thought of trying to filled me with fear.

The second anxiety eased as we drove into Nashville. Something about the skyscrapers – more sparse than in New York, here they had room to breathe amid a clear blue sky. Human endeavour plus nature's infinity: Who wouldn't feel inspired? And this was after all the capital of country. I put on a country compilation that I could tell even Jake secretly enjoyed. Bob did a "Yee-ha!" and I thought: Of course I'll write more songs.

The show was good too, the crowd friendly and up-for-it in a way you just don't get in sceptical, jaded London. But then we ended up doing tequila slammers with the local support act who turned out not to be very interesting after all. So I began our first day off in a fortnight with a hangover. It was the sort of mistake I was supposed to have grown out of.

Jake and I set out across town with a vague plan of finding a famous vintage guitar shop, not that we could afford to buy much. We were trudging up a hill under an oppressive sun when I foolishly shared with him the second anxiety.

"Maybe you're a genius after all," said Jake, not nicely. "Maybe that's why you've got writer's block. Because you're a genius."

"Well, where's *your* hit single?" He could be a dick; I could be a dick. "I keep waiting for it, but it's not happening for you either, is it?"

He pushed on ahead of me. His waist above his jeans looked doughy, the famous Delta Bloat taking its toll. (So the portions are bigger? Just leave half.) Jake had also forgotten his baseball cap and I could see the skin turning pink beneath his thinning hair.

He turned round. "Maybe you should go solo, see how you find that. You could stay here, become a genuine, bona fide, honest-to-God *country* singer."

I tried to steer us back onto safer territory.

"You know you should just surrender to the country, Jake. It's such a relief when you give in. Face it, country *rocks*."

But when he turned round again, he looked angry. "Are we having musical differences? Because ..."

He was cut off by a familiar-sounding whistle. We'd arrived at a railway line. The train approached at

31

an easy pace and took a good five minutes to roll by, plenty of time for us to admire the graffiti. I liked the way that no-one had bothered to wash it off, as if there were a tacit agreement between the vandal-artists and the rail company. This was Union Pacific Railroad, which reminded me of the Westerns I'd watched as a kid. Another magical, American touch. I looked over at Jake and saw he was almost smiling now, half-glancing at me. I sat down on a patch of grass and after a minute he sat beside me as the train rumbled and creaked its way past. When it had gone Jake held out a hand. I shook it. He got to his feet and yanked me up after him. The silence that followed as we walked on I think you could almost call companionable.

Then I saw the black building with one red door and one yellow door, and the sign, THIRD MAN RECORDS.

"Hey, I've heard about this," I said. "It's Jack White's."

"What is it, a record shop?"

"Yeah, but it's, like, his record label. He might be there now."

"I'm not in the mood to meet Jack White. I'm gonna scout ahead for lunch. Call me when you're finished."

That seemed like a good idea. And if he was going to sneak a quick beer, so what? We didn't have a show that night. I went in. The staff were all beautiful women. So not your typical record shop. Maybe this added to my sense of disquiet, a tinnitus-like ring of anxiety. What was it really about? Writer's block? Resentment over the vast talent and wealth and general coolness of Jack White? I was about to leave empty-handed when a bloke stumbled out of a photo booth-type-thing.

"Woah, check this out," he said. He wore a cheap Tanglewood guitar, strings rattling, a cowboy hat, sweaty Jack Daniels t-shirt. "I'm cuttin' a record here."

Yes, there was beer on his breath, but his expectation that I should be friendly was disarming.

"This here booth is like a miniature recording studio. You put your money in here, and when this light goes red? You're rocking. Here's mine." He held up a 7-inch in its paper sleeve. "I suck on this. I suck in general but hey, it's fun to play, right? I'm Sandy." He held out a hand. Before I knew what I was doing, I'd paid my fifteen dollars and was standing in the booth with Sandy's Tanglewood round my neck, facing the red light.

I played *The Sweetest Pain,* which calmed me down a bit. Partly because it reminded me of Amanda and it always will. In the early days, I'd get sore and she'd ask if I was okay to carry on. Yes, I'd say, because the soreness was *good* pain. The *sweetest* pain. In the song, it's ostensibly a reference to that line in *Romeo and Juliet* about parting being such sweet sorrow. But for me and Amanda it was always a lovers' dirty joke. Anyway. It was a good song. And who's to say even better stuff didn't lie ahead? I was 33, probably younger than Springsteen when he wrote *Born in the USA.* Twenty-eight years younger than Cohen when he wrote *Hallelujah.*

Sandy and I listened to the playback. It sounded like something from the 20s. It sounded like a piece of history.

"Kiss my ass if that ain't great. What're you, some kind of musician?"

I told him the name of the band, invited him to come to our show the next night, offered to put him on the guest list, and left with a feeling that this was a great country. I've still got that record somewhere.

Jake had been for a couple of soothing beers and was in a good mood when I found him. I went to the bar and ordered a nachos for us to share, plus a diet coke for me.

When he saw the coke, Jake put on his hillbilly voice. "Well, if it ain't the soda-pop kid ..."

"It's three in the afternoon," I said.

Still as the hillbilly: "Hell, it's five o'clock somewhere."

This was a line from an Alan Jackson song I'd played him, which of course he'd been snarky about. I took his use of it as a concession to country, or America or maybe just me, and ordered a beer with the next round. A band was setting up. Two girls - women I should say; they were at least my age - one on mandolin

35

and one on guitar, and a bloke on double-bass. The mandolin girl (I'm just going to call them girls, okay?) wore a hat, cut-off jeans and boots, golden hair and golden thighs flashing in the sunlight that streamed in through the windows and onto the stage. The guitar girl was lanky with a sleek brown bob, black jeans and a blouse. They seemed to clash, but then when they tested the mics their harmonies were beautiful. The double bassist was a balding blonde guy with a full beard and an open waistcoat. Which one's boyfriend was he? Often these acts involve a couple, but there was something, not unfriendly but *chaste* about the way they set up and tuned up together. Then he said something to them both and the mandolin girl laughed, head thrown back, breasts thrust forward, while guitar girl rolled her eyes.

"Hey Soda-pop!" Jake was waving to me, not caring that his fake hillbilly accent could be heard above the twang of the mandolin. "A man could die of thirst around here."

I carried the beers back to the table.

They were the best band I'd seen for ages. The songs were world-weary, unlucky-in-love stuff, sad and funny. The girls' voices coiled around each other and blended gorgeously. They were great with the audience as well. It was a semi-distracted, late-afternoon crowd. But the band soon grabbed their attention.

"This is song about fading passion," said the guitar girl.

"Passion fades?" said the bassist.

"It does for some of us, sweetheart."

"I thought it was because you didn't want the commitment right now."

Then the mandolin girl chimed in. "Y'all are still in therapy, right?" To the crowd: "See how weird it gets with these two? Can you imagine sharing a tour bus with these guys? I mean I love them and all. But still -"

"Did she say she loves me? Things are looking up, boys."

Then the guitar girl, eyes to the ceiling, sighed. "Declan, we trusted you with that microphone. Now honour that trust. This song's called *Fading Lights*. I have no idea why I wrote it."

It was impossible to tell how much of this was scripted. I watched the guitar girl and the bassist, thinking that this was the way to be with your ex - self-deprecating, harmlessly bantering in public, older and wiser but not bitter.

It became clear that the songs were written by guitar girl, and as each one went by I'd be chasing it, trying to figure out what made it work so well, how it could be satisfyingly predictable and yet full of surprises, how the lyrics could be so simple and yet profound. Then there was the obligatory curve-ball cover: *Friends in Low Places* by Garth Brooks, which they turned from a defiantly laddish drinking anthem into a mournful tale of heartbreak. It made me wonder if that was how *Friends in Low Places* had been intended, before Garth got his chubby mitts on it.

After the set they carried their gear out, then Declan headed to the bar. The girls came over and joined a foursome on the opposite side of our table, just out of earshot as piped music started up. I turned to Jake.

"I loved that," I said. But he was staring across the table with a look I knew very well. He was staring, of course, at Mandolin Girl. Then he lunged across the table and I heard him shout, "That was bloody marvellous. May I buy you girls a drink?"

He'd poshed-up his accent, either for the sake of trans-Atlantic clarity or to impress them with a Hugh Grant act.

Mandolin Girl looked like she might be considering it, struck by this handsome bloke looming at her, but Guitar Girl shook her head, pointing at the bar, where Declan was loading a tray with beers. As Jake sat back I caught Guitar Girl's eye, tried to convey something of my musical admiration in a nod, which she seemed to interpret as intended.

"Stuck-up cow," said Jake, and I got up and walked around the table. I hovered awkwardly until I got Guitar Girl's attention – the hint of alarm in her almond-shaped eyes, the smell of shampoo on her brown bob. I babbled something, trying to get across how good I thought they were, and also that this should mean something to her as I was a musician myself and so knew what I was talking about. You can believe me or not, but at the time I wanted nothing more than for her to understand that her talent was genuine. That's all any of us want, we musicians. Like I said, you can believe me or not.

"Thank you," she said. "Now sit down. You're making me nervous."

More beers were placed in front of us. I went to the restroom and pissed hurriedly and at one point I went to the bar, but mostly I was sitting very close to Colette, talking about music and love. I was aware that over her shoulder Jake was now snogging Mandolin Girl. I kept seeing his pale hand stroking her thigh, on which tiny golden hairs shone, just beneath the high hem of her cut-off jeans.

Colette was born in Texas and had moved to Nashville to pursue her music eight years ago. As we talked I heard myself in contrast to her easy drawl – less pronounced than Mandolin Girl's twang, but definitely there, about two notches down from Gina Davis in *Thelma and Louise*. I had a go at her accent and she had a go at mine, and we agreed that I could do hers much better.

I showed her my record, and she said she'd intended to cut one herself, but hadn't got round to it. She asked about Amanda and I told her a fair bit.

"So she doesn't understand you, right?" she said. She looked at me steadily as she sipped her beer.

"Are you taking the piss?"

"What's that? You mean am I fucking with you? No, I'm not. It just sounds like she doesn't understand what it's like for musicians. For artists in general."

That was a scary thought. I tried to keep it light, explaining Amanda's failure to get the Alan Partridge gag about the best Beatles album.

"Okay, I get it," she said, smiling. "But you know what a better question is? What's your *favourite* Beatles album?"

"Yes. And what's yours?"

"Whichever one has *Eight Days a Week* on it. Because that just sounds like being in love."

I shook my head. "You're so ..."

"Don't say cool," she laughed. "I am *not* cool."

She put her glass down, lay her hand on my shoulder and leaned in.

"Okay, okay." Declan loomed over us. His eyes looked bloodshot and the veins in his long neck bulged. The loveable doofus he'd been on stage was gone. "I'm getting out of here, Col."

"You're sure?"

"Why the hell would I stay?" His head nodded towards me but his gaze remained locked on her.

"Music? Beer?"

"Fuck you."

She winced, more in sorrow than anger, refusing, I thought, to give up on him. "I'm sorry, Declan."

"Yeah right. So I guess you want me to pack up all your shit, too."

"We loaded up already. Remember? Are you okay? I mean, are you sure you're okay to drive?"

"Am I okay to drive? What do you care? You know sometimes you sound just like a pain-in-the-ass *wife*. So I guess I got the worst of both worlds." He looked down at me. "Enjoy the special relationship," he said.

When he'd gone she gave me a sad smile.

"We were engaged. I broke it off. I guess that would do it, right?"

I put my hand on her back. It was the first time I touched her and I was surprised at the sharpness of her shoulder blade. She squeezed my thigh, raised her beer. "To the special relationship."

The next act started up, a young, too-screechy blues singer drowning himself out with a muddy slide guitar.

"So can your band survive this thing with you and Declan?" I asked.

Colette shrugged, looking quite tough. "Probably not, but I have plenty of other ideas. Anyway -" Her lips on my ear. "Come back to my apartment?"

We shared a cab. I took the front seat, at one point turning to see Jake and Mandolin Girl still going at it. Pressed up against the door by Mandolin's arse, Collette gave me such an understated look of stoical endurance that I laughed. Jake came up for air.

"Jake, we leave at ten tomorrow."

"I'll be there."

"Shake on it."

I reached round and we shook hands. Jake gave a slight nod to Collette, a complicit wink.

Colette's apartment was on a busy street among bars and shops. I followed her narrow back up a flight of stairs. As she unlocked the door I came up behind her and kissed her neck, her clever, musician's ears.

"Okay, but first I want to show you something."

We stepped into her apartment. Sparse furnishings. *The New York Times*, a couple of novels, and general mess strewn around the place. "Okay, so I'm a mess, but I wasn't expecting you." She pointed at me. "Hey! Potential song idea!" She dumped her leather jacket. "Make yourself at home."

I sat down while she produced a bottle of Jack Daniels, shot glasses and a bottle of Coke.

She plucked an acoustic guitar from its stand and strummed a few chords. *Eight Days a Week*. She was on the *hold me, love me* bit when she paused at a seventh chord. "Now that," she said, "is fucking genius." She flipped the guitar over and thrust it into my hands. "Show me what you can do."

"Shit. This feels like a test."

"Don't worry. I'm just going to sit here, quietly judging you. Coke?" She was pouring Jack Daniels into two shot glasses on the coffee table that sat between us.

"No thanks."

I played *The Sweetest Pain* for the second time that day. When I'd finished, she said, "It's great. I'm relieved. I mean, what if you sucked? What then?"

The question would have to wait because she had stood up and was stepping towards me, unbuttoning her blouse.

What makes great sex? I think we can agree that it at least partly depends on what's going through your mind at the time. Unless you think the mind should be blank. Is that what makes it great? The obliteration of thought by sensation? Well, my mind was not blank while I had sex with Colette.

Some things I thought about:

One: Jarvis Cocker. The Pulp singer, I remember, was once asked what sort of girls he liked. His reply was that he tended to go for the fuller figure, partly because he himself was thin. Jarvis with a thin girl, he said, was 'like two skeletons fighting in the dark'. Jarvis's most memorable line, unfortunately.

Two: Colette and her talent. The wit, wisdom and compassion that I'd heard in her songs and her conversation. How much I respected, admired and liked her.

Three: Jake's hand sliding up Mandolin's golden thigh.

Four: Jenna, the goth girl, standing with her robe open, staring at me and sticking out her tongue.

Five: Amanda.

The first of these I thought about because it related to my current difficulty; the second because I hoped it would help me with that difficulty, the third and fourth because they actually did help with the difficulty, and the fifth because I couldn't help it.

Anyway, it happened. And afterwards it felt good to lie in her arms.

"Would you have still had sex with me if I'd sucked?" I was trying out the American bluntness with matters sexual.

She gave a salty laugh. "Yeah, I probably would've done. Because you're cute and I like you. But … I dunno, it's funny … maybe I wouldn't have enjoyed it as much."

"Glad you enjoyed it."

"And you?"

"God, yeah. I think you're bloody great."

"And yet ..." She kissed me lightly on the lips, looked into my eyes. The evening light coming in through her window lightened her brown irises, turning them yellow. "It's just that this isn't exactly a passion raging beyond your control now, is it?"

I started to protest.

"Shh. It's okay." She kissed me again, put her head on my chest. "I can settle for being bloody great."

I stroked her hair. I heard the faint thud of music from the bar down the road, and beyond that, the whistle of the freight train.

"The lonesome whistle," she said. "In songs it's always a lonesome whistle, but for me, it makes me feel less alone."

"You know you're wrong about one thing, Colette. You *are* cool."

She sighed. "I know."

Next morning, as I pulled on my new cowboy boots, Colette sat on the edge of the couch strumming her guitar.

"Are you getting my oh-so-subtle message here?"

I realised the song was *You're Gonna Make Me Lonesome When You Go.*

"Me too," I said.

She put the guitar down and we kissed.

I grabbed her arse, said, "Stop it, or you're gonna make me late."

She smiled. "Yeah right. Hey, you'll look me up next time you're in Nashville, right?"

"Sure. I'll miss you." It was true.

She was kissing, then biting my neck, quite hard. She laughed wickedly. "I've tagged you. You're *mine*, dude. Return the favour?" She pulled up her top. "Down here. We don't want to upset Declan more than is strictly necessary."

I got down on my knees, found a bite of spare flesh and sucked it through my teeth.

"Something to remember me by," I said when I'd finished.

"Something by which to remember me," she said in an English accent. As herself: "Now get outta here." She handed me my record. "And don't forget this."

I was drinking coffee in the lobby with an anxious Bob when Jake reeled in at ten-forty. He was flushed with sunburn and last night's drink. His T-shirt was on inside out. Perched on his head, backwards, was Mandolin's Stetson. He shot me a look of complicity which made me hate myself.

Jimi Hendrix on tour, according to legend: He'd arrive in a city and walk around until he found a guitar shop. He'd go in, maul a couple of Strats and choose one for that night's show. The Strat would end up either trashed on stage – smashed to pieces or maybe drenched in gasoline and burned alive – or he'd give it away or simply leave it behind. Then, guitarless and unencumbered, he'd hit the town: *Freedom!* He'd end up having sex with one or more girls and crashing where his head hit the pillow, couch or carpet. (Or did the world's greatest guitarist sometimes just pass out between a woman's thighs?) The manager, Chas Chandler, faced the headache each morning of finding Hendrix, who could be anywhere in the city, and getting him the hell on the road.

Is it facile to draw parallels between the way Hendrix treated women and the way he treated guitars? One thing's for sure: I am no Jimi Hendrix. And I'm still strumming the same Telecaster my mum gave me on my 18th birthday.

On the flight home, I tried to read the *Washington Post*, and gave up when I hit on the phrase 'renovations would ruin the historic building's architectural integrity'. From then on, I had the word 'integrity' going round and round in my head like a Mika single. I'd never given it much thought before, and only appreciated its value now it was gone. It was as if I'd left a piece of myself in that apartment in Nashville, and now had to come home, deformed and incomplete, to face the miserable and unachievable task of trying to bullshit the love of my life into believing that nothing had changed.

Amanda opened the door, fell into my arms.

"I've missed you," she said. We kissed. Then she stopped, held me at arm's length, the colour draining from her face.

*

The official version is that our band was killed by the internet. And it's true that no-one sells CDs any more. Unless you're Take That, Adele, or indeed that famous alt-country cross-over artist, Colette Jones. But there were other factors – the deterioration of my song-writing, Jake's drugs problems and declining looks. I felt sorry for myself, of course, and for Jake, most of the time, but also for Bob who'd probably now never get another chance. So when the label went under and he called to ask for my help in moving out of the boxy office-cum-kitchen at the Kilburn premises, it was the least I could do.

"Okay, so it's a shit sandwich," said Bob. "But we've got to eat it. How about a beer to wash it down with? It's five o'clock somewhere."

"I'd better not." I had a late shift at the British Gas call centre.

"Right, this box here is a load of crap that we've accumulated over the years. Photos, clippings, various demos and stuff. The way I'm doing it, this pile is stuff to chuck, this pile is stuff to keep, this pile is stuff to sell."

We began sorting through the box. I remembered doing this as I moved out of the house I'd shared with Amanda, the incessant decisions, the buffeting of memories and regrets.

"Woah. Jake with hair."

He held up an early picture. Yes, Jake looked gorgeous. But my gaze quickly sought my younger self, as it always does in moments like this. I tried to remember how it felt to be so slim, and to not have tinnitus.

"Chuck it," I said.

He put it on the junk pile and upended a box of CDs. We began to rummage.

"Are you still in touch?"

"Not really."

The last few times I'd seen Jake had followed the same pattern. We'd go out for a drink or a meal, and I'd try to pretend that I hadn't noticed that he was already smashed. Then he'd get soppy, then he'd ask me for money, and I'd refuse, and he'd get nasty, and I'd have to help him home. The most recent time, I realised he was smashed, had one drink and left.

I was trying to decide whether or not to keep a CD on which was written *The Sweetest Pain extended mix*, wondering if, under the straitened circumstances, it might be wiser just to eBay it – we still had fans who lapped up what was left of our memorabilia - when Bob said, "Hey, what's this? It's from the US. Nashville." He looked at me with some sympathy as well as pity. "Don't worry. They'll be inundated with stuff. They probably never listened to it."

"I never sent a demo to Nashville," I said.

He didn't believe me. "Well, Nashville sent one to you." He tossed it over.

But the package was not CD-shaped. The writing was elaborate with a certain elegance at the expense of legibility. And female. I opened it. It was a record, a 7-inch single on whose sleeve was written: "This recording was performed live inside the THIRD MAN RECORD BOOTH."

In Bob's pile of shit to sell was a record player. I moved it to the counter and plugged it in. My hands were shaky as I lowered the needle. There was the familiar retro-sounding fizz and crackle, then a springy, major-key waltz strummed on a capo'd acoustic. Then the voice.

"He said would you still love me if my music sucked? / I said I don't know but I'm glad that we ... f-ell

down together, and I lay in your arms / Now there's a bite on my belly and an ache in my heart ...”

"Bloody hell," said Bob. "Colette."

It was her alright. The same voice that was now famous. But it was also lighter; you could tell she was smiling as she sang.

"And I hope you find love / And I hope you stay free / Well here's something by which to remember me ..."

Afterwards, Bob said, "Did she ever release that?"

I shook my head.

"So she wrote that just for you?"

I nodded, cleared my throat. "Bob, I think I'll have that beer after all."

"Good man." On his way to the fridge, he lowered the needle again. We listened and drank. When it was over, he said, "That must have taken her ages."

"Not really. Don't forget she's very talented."

I got up and placed the record back in its flimsy sleeve.

"Sell or keep? You realise that's worth a lot now."

"Keep," I said, and placed it carefully in the box. This was one test I was determined not to fail.

Thirteen o'Clock

Which was the worst part of being abandoned – the cancellation of her future or the rewriting of her past?

Sophie stood in the doorway of her daughter's bedroom. The child was standing on one leg while Sophie's mother delved into the pack of wet-wipes and dabbed at that awkward bit where the buttocks met the thigh.

"Oh, *there* you are," said Florence.

"Sorry. I must have been tired. Thanks for –"

But now Florence addressed her granddaughter, stuffing the soiled wet-wipes into a nappy bag. "Mummy will take over now."

"Thanks for letting me sleep, Mum."

"You looked like you needed it."

Sophie's mother found some clothes in the drawer

and laid them on the bed.

"I was going to put her in jeans."

"*Much* too warm for jeans," said Florence on her way out.

Through the window streamed the light of a bright, August day, casting a halo around Nell's golden curls as she made little jumps on the bed. Sophie was struck by how beautiful her daughter was. Then the moment was lost in the familiar fog of exhaustion.

Sophie's body performed the tasks – getting Nell still enough to apply the fresh nappy, pants, vest, dress, keeping up the stream of commentary and nuzzling her daughter's naked belly to make her laugh. The ache in her lower back was beginning to nag again. The clock on the bedside table said nine-thirty-six. She'd been up with Nell only once in the night. It was enough. Since her husband left she'd been in a chronic state of exhaustion, as if the shock of finding herself abandoned took up all her energy. Or maybe this was simply how it felt to be nearly 36.

Radio Two could be heard from the kitchen, its home-on-a-weekday prattle lowering her spirits. As soon as she'd heard about Andy leaving, Florence had dropped everything - her recently retired, possibly depressed husband, her busy round of social commitments - to rush to her daughter's rescue. She made the journey from Birmingham to Leeds every weekend and stayed for three nights at a time. But talking with her had never been easy. Sophie tried anyway, the night Florence arrived, depleting a bottle of Pinot Grigio under her mother's baleful gaze.

"It's like the ground beneath me has fallen through," she said, "and I'm just, like, plunging down and down."

Florence began fussing at the sink. "Well, what you need to do is control the controllables. I mean, when did you last dust the shelves in the spare room? And when are you going to sort out the loft?"

Was Sophie imagining the accusation implicit in her mother's words – that Andy had left because she was a lousy wife?

Some basic facts: They'd married three years ago, had the baby a year later. Before Nell was one Andy began an affair with a younger woman he met through –

well, 'work' would have to be the word. Now he'd abandoned Sophie and was living in a flat in London with his new woman. He said he still wanted to be part of their lives, whatever that meant. It was a common tale. And one she'd found herself sharing with the headteacher of the secondary school at which she taught English. Emily Hackett had called her into the office having had 'some concerns' regarding Sophie's recent performance and general demeanour.

A hot fist was trying to push its way up from Sophie's heart and into her throat. Sophie resorted to the vernacular of those women's magazines the cleaner left hanging around in the staffroom. "I married a Love Rat. Okay? But the thing is, Emily, until we'd had the baby and it was too late, he didn't *seem* like a Love Rat."

She'd never had a heart-to-heart with the headteacher before, but then she was having a lot of conversations for the first time. Emily Hackett's eyes softened. "They never do, Sophie." But then she added, "So I'm told."

The headteacher, by the way, was one year younger than Sophie. On her desk was a framed family portrait. It featured Emily, a charming poppet and one of those paunchy-but-competent-looking blokes with a bald head that looked solid as varnished oak.

Once, Sophie would not have looked twice at a man like that. She used to have a thing for artistically talented blokes. She liked that mysterious creativity that elevated them above the mundane. She liked their floppy hair, their impassioned monologues and glittering eyes. She met Andy at her writers' group. The days when she believed she could make any sort of living out of her poetry were long gone. But she'd continued to write, and wanted to meet like-minded people. Okay, and possibly a like-minded bloke.

Andy wrote sci-fi, which in hindsight should have put her off. For Sophie, sci-fi was too detached from real life, loved by men who never quite grew up, who secretly longed to be Luke Skywalker – and for you to be Princess Leia. But Andy was handsome. When, after one of the group's critique sessions, he invited her for a drink at the pub across the street, she felt flattered.

She was going through a confident phase, and told him what she thought about his chosen genre. He wasn't having it, naturally.

"Sci-fi is *absolutely* committed to exploring the real world," he declared. "It just does so in an oblique way. All great art does that. It doesn't simply reflect life, it portrays it refracted, contorted, defamiliarised."

Oh, he could talk the talk alright.

"But that story of yours tonight," she said. "It was *such* a parallel universe that it seemed too childish. I mean, what are those female creatures with fluffy tails and fury breasts?"

He blushed. "Mammarians."

"I can't take them seriously. Sorry."

Sophie made a point in those days of *not* telling an attractive bloke exactly what she thought he wanted to hear. But in avoiding one mistake, was she now making another? Andy looked crushed.

"You said you admired *Nineteen-Eighty-Four*," he reminded her. "That's sci-fi."

"Yes, but that's so politically committed. And well written." She couldn't stop herself. "I mean, remember the first line? *It was a bright, cold day in April and the clocks were striking thirteen.* Write something like that."

"Sure. Excuse me one moment while I pull a literary classic out of my arse." And he mimed doing so, making a grotesque sucking sound with his lips and then pretending to lay his 'classic' on the table in front of her. He was a convincing mime, and it made her laugh. But then he glanced about, fidgeting.

"You don't like me anymore."

He looked at her with his bright, long-lashed eyes, and something turned over in her chest.

"I do, actually, Sophie. I like a woman who speaks her mind." Yes, he actually said that. She should have got it in writing. "And I enjoyed that poem you read tonight. It was very sweet."

And Sophie, like a fool, was filled with a warm glow of validation.

Andy could feign artistic arrogance, but she knew that he too wanted validation. He *was* his writing. If she didn't love *it*, did she love *him*? But it didn't seem right that he was the one who demanded to be taken seriously. Because he honestly wasn't any good. At first.

She tried, but she just couldn't get along with his furry-breasted aliens. By the time they were married, he'd stopped showing her his stuff. He showed it instead to fellow sci-fi nerds in internet chatrooms. He was *always* on the computer. So she didn't notice, until it was too late, that he'd become good. Somewhere during her second trimester, his third novel was snapped up by an agent. When Nell was four months old, it was taken on by a publisher. Then suddenly he was having to take the train down to London while the domestic drudgery fell to her.

One Saturday she came home early from a children's party. He was in the loo. She heard him calling her name, sounding anxious. Compelled by an obscure instinct, she sat down at his computer. She shook the mouse, banishing the screen saver of a comic-book alien space ship, and began to read his emails. The toilet flushed. Andy emerged, drying his hands on his sleeves. She looked at him and he turned white.

Ursula Birch held a lowly position at a literary agency. It was she who discovered Andy's novel in the slush pile. He told Sophie this, making a point.

"Does she have furry tits?" Sophie asked.

"No, she doesn't," Andy said, shaking his head. "No, in fact they're lovely and smooth."

Sophie found Ursula Birch on Facebook, saw a short, plump girl whose sex appeal lay in her wide, red mouth and mischievous eyes thickly decorated in gothy makeup. On her profile picture, she gazed up at Andy while he brandished a copy of his novel. Ursula Birch was of course a total sci-fi nerd. There were pictures of her posing with Stormtroopers and Ewoks at some ghastly *Star Wars* convention.

She agonised over the early mistake she made of not giving him a wide berth; she ruminated constantly about his abandonment of her; but her mind recoiled from some of the episodes in between - the proposal, the wedding, the honeymoon. Days could pass when she wondered if she'd ever been in love with him. Now it seemed she woke up every day in a parallel universe, where Andy was gone, Nell was crying and the clocks were striking thirteen.

She ate half of the huge fry-up Florence had made for her, trying not to dwell on how screwed up it was that her mother seemed to be trying to thwart her efforts to lose weight. Nell upended a bowl of porridge and waved it about at arm's length. Gobs of grey cement-mix spattered onto the table, the floor, and into the hard-to-reach nooks of the plastic high chair that was such a drag to clean because Andy had been too tight to buy a decent one that time she'd made the mistake of trusting him with a trip to Ikea ...

"Are you alright?"

Sophie was toiling on the kitchen floor with a cloth. She looked up at Florence's concerned expression, realised that her cheeks were hot and wet and her breathing came in thick gasps.

Florence took the cloth from her.

"You go and get dressed. We'll watch CBeebies for a bit, won't we, Nell? While Mummy pulls herself together."

Upstairs she sat on the bed and got her breathing

under control. Then she put on a size-twelve dress she'd only recently been able to fit back into. She went to work on her face. Her first boyfriend had told her that crying made her look hot. Well, that was then. The dress, though, was an irrefutable triumph. She almost smiled as she imagined a celebrity magazine headline: *Sophie: Slim, single, and sexier than ever.*

She checked her phone. John Parks, the bloke she'd been messaging, confirming that he was still on for their date. Don't get excited, she told herself, brushing a clump of congealed porridge from her hair.

She stepped outside with Nell. The air was cool, the sun warm on her face. Her spirits lifted at the prospect, however illusory, of escape. The feeling persisted while she grappled with the clasps of Nell's car seat, struggling to get the pins into a socket crammed with rice-cake crumbs while her lower back ached. Then Nell was in, and smiling at her.

"You're beautiful," she said, tickling her ribs and loving the way Nell immediately squirmed and giggled. One of the few predictable things in life: you tickle Nell,

67

she laughs.

She snapped a selfie and uploaded it to Facebook with the caption: "Glorious day! Off out for quality time with my little angel." Maybe that was how you made yourself happy - you simply told everyone how happy you were.

As she drove through the countryside to Harrogate she reminded herself that she still had two weeks left of the summer holiday. But already the leaves were gaining an autumnal tinge. She switched on the radio. *Woman's Hour.* Jane Garvey introducing an item about women who had "found love in later life and were more emotionally – and sexually – fulfilled than ever." Sophie turned it up, feeling neglected cogs of her mind beginning to creak into life. But Nell was trying to speak. After a couple of goes, Sophie was able to interpret her splutter as a request for her CD. She put it on. *The Wheels on the Bus.*

"Mummy sing! Mummy sing!"

So she sang. Round and round. Round and round. All day fucking long.

In the play gym she found a table, changed Nell's nappy in the toilet, then let her loose on the ball pool. Two hours had passed since John Parks's message. Enough suspense. She replied: *Great. See you at 8. Xxx.* Were the kisses too much? What did *she* know about these things? While she was out of the game, the rules had changed. Once you simply met someone; now you were a commodity to be cynically marketed.

But it wasn't hard to find men, if you cast your net wide enough. Dozens had been in touch since she set up her profile. John Parks was the first who'd seemed worth a date. According to his profile he was quite the action man, claiming to enjoy 'abseiling, climbing and scuba-diving'. She pictured herself with John Parks, following a day of outdoor adventure, returning to a log fire in a countryside hotel, then heading upstairs to the bedroom where he'd -

"Mummy mummy mummy -"

Nell was grabbing her hand. Sophie allowed herself to be dragged between the tables towards a kid-

69

sized vending machine selling chocolate eggs.

"It'll put you off your lunch."

Nell's face screwed up into an evil-looking ball, her socked feet stomping on the coffee-stained carpet tiles.

"*No*," said Sophie.

Nell sat down, face upturned as if appealing for mercy from a sadistic God. She filled her lungs and screamed. Sophie gathered her up – the thrashing torso, the flailing legs – and got her back to the table. She lifted her and smelled her nappy, detecting only a tolerable urine reek. Then she bent over, holding Nell from behind on her lap, and dived for the change bag. She found the still-warm bottle. She plugged the teat into her daughter's mouth and propped her in her lap. A moment's contentment: crisis averted, order restored. Sophie put her head back and inhaled, smelling burnt coffee, grilling cheese and, wafting from the open door of the toilets, the faint, forgiveable tang of baby shit. She opened her eyes. Someone had left a women's magazine on the table. The romances, pregnancies and weight fluctuations of celebrities were reported with first-name familiarity. These people seemed to spend all their time on holiday, being photographed unawares. Sophie recognised about half of them, and succumbed to that state of anxious prurience that these magazines always induced. Some of the pictures had the women's imperfections circled in white. Mostly to do with body fat, sometimes body hair. She pushed the magazine out of reach. Who read this stuff? Why had she even looked at it? Would she never learn?

Nell squirmed in her lap. Hunger sated and the chocolate vending machine mercifully forgotten, she was eager to get back to the play gym. Sophie let her go.

A young, bearded bloke three tables away was staring at her. Sophie caught his eye and he looked away. She sipped her coffee. She'd never had a bearded lover. What must it feel like? Four months now, since she'd had sex.

Now the bearded guy was coming over.

"Excuse me, love." He had a hard accent. Northern Irish? "Sorry to bother you."

"It's fine," she said, looking up. He was tall in his tight, white T-shirt. His body was strong-looking but uneven and fleshy in places, suggesting rugby or manual labour rather than jogging and the gym. Sophie, intimidated by the blackness of his eyes, darted her gaze downwards to the tattooed arms crossed over his chest. How would it feel to be enfolded in their embrace?

"Is that your little girl?" He pointed at Nell, who was pushing a ball around a rubber-walled enclosure.

"Yes." Sophie tucked a strand of hair behind her ear, expecting a compliment.

"She's lost one of her socks."

"Oh. So she has." Sophie glanced about, not finding the sock. "Thanks, I'll – I'll have a look for it..."

There was an intensity to his gaze now. "Can you read?" it sounded like he said.

"I'm sorry?"

Can *I* read? Did he want the magazine? She offered him it, but he was pointing at something, a sign on the wall:

"POLITE NOTICE: Parents' and carers' are kindly reminded to remove their childrens' shoes. Socks' / tights' must be worn at all time's."

72

"Oh. I see." She felt the burn of humiliation on her face. "Sorry."

"There are reasons for these rules," the man said. He shrugged and smiled, brilliant white teeth flashing in his black beard. Then, with insulting delicacy, he stepped aside as if to ease Sophie's passage from the table.

Sophie pushed herself to her feet, knocking her cup off the table. It bounced under a nearby chair. A woman yelped and jumped up, her tattooed ankles spattered with coffee.

"Sorry!" Sophie waved at a passing waitress. "Spilt something over here!"

Sophie pushed her way through the tables to the play gym. For a moment she couldn't see her daughter at all, then found her, back in the ball pool. She had to wait while Nell slipped down the slide, bare foot squeaking against the plastic.

"Come on! Chocolate time!"

Nell, turning her back, said, "Slide."

Sophie reached in to grab Nell below the arms.

73

Nell squirmed and Sophie yanked her, the child's scream of protest seeming for a second to express of the jolt of pain in Sophie's lower back. She pulled her out of the ball pool and stood, holding her against her chest. She angled her head away, protecting her ears against Nell's wailing. With her head back she couldn't see where she was going and stumbled over a wandering child. Nell took advantage of her mother's loosened grip and tried to slide down her body, but Sophie got the girl onto her hip, holding her like a battering ram as she waded through the other parents and careening toddlers.

She reached the table and began to clamp on Nell's shoes. Nell was squirming so much that Sophie had no choice but to lie her on her back in order to fasten them. Nell began a side-to-side writhing, like an epileptic (was she epileptic?) and succeeded in clanging her temple against the leg of a chair. Sophie let the child scream and let people watch while she yanked on her jacket, stuffed Nell's jacket into the change bag, shouldered the change bag, then picked up her screaming daughter and marched to the exit with Nell held aloft like a sacrificial offering.

Twenty minutes later they were half-way back to Leeds and Nell was asleep, lolling forward against the straps like dead fighter pilot. Sophie pulled into a lay-by next to an empty field and snapped off *Dingle Dangle Scarecrow*. Silence: cars rushing by at 60, a thin drizzle beginning to patter the windscreen. Pain gnawed her lower spine and a band tightened around her temples. She delved in the glove compartment for drugs. She found some Ibuprofen and necked a couple, then a deliciously prohibited third. She was re-stashing them when her phone buzzed.

Thinking, despite herself, of Andy, she fumbled in her bag so hastily that she opened the attachment before seeing who had sent it. Then she realised that the man who was lying, trouserless on a bed, his semi-hard-on concealed by his tight white pants, a leering grin on his bearded face – was John Parks, her date for that night.

The caption said, "Looking forward to seeing you in the flesh."

What she did next, she did deliberately without

thought. She kicked off her shoes, put one foot on the seat, slipped off her bra and pulled her dress down, exposing one breast. She took eight pictures, chose the best one. Her bare thighs looked fleshy but not without shape; the folds of her dress concealed the remains of her baby bulge; her raised arms elevated her not-what-they-used-to-be breasts, and her expression looked far more confident than she felt. She sent the picture. Then she thrust her phone into her bag and started the car, pulling away like someone fleeing the scene of a crime.

The sky continued to darken, clouds casting shadows over the fields on either side of the downward-sloping road. Sophie's bare foot pushed down the accelerator. The speedometer nudged up to 60 and beyond. Sophie pictured the headteacher stopping her in the corridor. Emily Hackett would have that 'concerned' look, the dainty crease between her eyes. "Can you come to my office after school?" In her office she would be joined by one of the assistant heads, sombrely poised to make notes. "There's no easy way to say this, Sophie," Emily might start. Or perhaps she'd just plunge in with, "I'm afraid the children have got hold of a picture that was posted online ..." The interview would conclude with recommendations that Sophie contact supply agencies, consider private tutoring, though of course she'd understand that under these regrettable circumstances the headteacher couldn't possibly be expected to provide a reference ...

Back home, Sophie and her mother got in each other's way as they prepared lunch. Asked why she was back so soon, Sophie tried to explain the effect on her of Sock Man incident. But halfway through she noticed her mother's eyes glaze over, and was hardly surprised when she said, "You know the problem is those silly little socks everyone seems to buy children these days. Children *will* pull those short socks off, which is why it's better to get the longer kind, even in summer."

By the time she'd finished eating, torpor was beginning to descend, and it was a huge relief when her mother offered to take Nell to the supermarket.

She woke to find a steaming cup of tea on the bedside table. She could hear in the living room below

Florence's voice in a grandmotherly sing-song, the gorgeous bubbling of Nell's laughter. She sat up and drank the tea, realising that her head felt clearer than it had done for days. And she looked better. Dressing for her date with John Parks, she composed a headline: *Single Sophie flaunts her post-baby bod and hunky beefcake beau...*

One of the many advantages enjoyed by men is that they're allowed to be early for a first date. They can choose a seat, enjoy a nerve-steadying drink, then watch you approach, giving you the full head-to-toe scrutiny while they sit, protected by the table. But what did Sophie know about modern sexual mores? Maybe nowadays it was the women who arrived early and it never entered their heads to think that made them look 'desperate'.

Anyway, she was five minutes late, and found John Parks comfortably installed in a booth, fiddling with his phone and nursing a pint of lager. He stood for a kiss on the cheek. She felt the tickle of his beard; her heart leapt at his male smell. She excused herself and went to the bar. Now he was no doubt checking out her arse. Should she have offered to buy him a drink? Stop it, she told herself. Be yourself, whatever that turns out to be these days.

In his steady, middle-class voice, he asked what she'd done that day and she told him, ending with the Sock Man anecdote. After the rehearsal on her mother, she'd got better at it, even felt emboldened to have a go at Sock Man's Irish accent. John Parks at least realised he was supposed to be amused and outraged.

"Nightmare!" he laughed. And if he was secretly thinking that she was a lousy mother and didn't want to see her again then so what?

She asked him about himself, and learned that his job was 'okay', he lived with two other blokes who were 'fine', and that he'd split with his ex-girlfriend because they 'grew apart'. When none of her questions elicited a fuller response, Sophie began to wonder if the whole drink-and-conversation part of the evening was a tedious ritual to be got out of the way before the shagging could start. But it was hard to know if she was reading this right. Part of the trouble was that she'd finished her large glass of Chardonnay and had another one bought for her, and the first drinks for a fortnight were clouding her brain.

"So what's drifting apart like?"

He shrugged. "Is this what we should be talking about? It's not allowed, is it? Going on about your ex on a first date?"

"What are we *supposed* to be talking about? Property prices? Bloody *Game of Thrones*?"

He smiled. "I think I like you."

She raised her wine; they clinked glasses.

"And I enjoyed your picture."

"Thanks." She looked away.

"Alright. There was this girl at work ..."

She put down her glass, hard. "You mean you cheated on her?"

"No."

"Liar."

"I was tempted. And it made me realise ..."

"You mean you got caught."

Was she really going to sabotage this date out of gender-based loyalty to a woman she'd never met?

80

He shrugged again, apparently not caring whether she believed him or not. Later she wondered if it was this indifference that attracted her. Was it the old bastards-are-sexy thing? You bash yourself against their armoured skins, failing to penetrate but bruising and cutting yourself until you're lying there, broken and bleeding. Then they calmly gobble you up and stroll on.

He was leaning towards her, conspiratorial. "So what's *your* story, Sophie? With your ex?"

Sophie was quite aware that some people, especially women's magazine writers, would caution against too much honesty at this point. She should probably have presented a drama-free narrative of conscious uncoupling. But Sophie was tired of not talking about this with her mother, the wine was coursing through her brain and she heard herself blurt, "He's a bastard. He's left me holding the baby while he's gone off to London to be a science fiction writer with a woman called Ursula Birch. That's how much our marriage meant to him."

His hand lay close to hers on the table and now he placed two fingers on her clenched fist. "And what did it mean to you, Sophie?"

By asking his questions, and looking into her eyes and nodding with what looked like compassion on his handsome face, he began to draw from her an account of Andy's proposal.

"We were on holiday in Croatia, staying in this hillside cottage. And there was a huge thunderstorm as we ran back from the restaurant up this massive hill, laughing and kissing in the rain. *Sooo* cheesy. Like something out of a bloody Richard Curtis film. Then we got back to the cottage and ..."

Sophie remembered making love as the lightning cast flashes over their skin, and the almost simultaneous thunder crashed around them like bombs. The next day they woke in the quiet of a still day, sunlight flooding the room, and they seemed to open their eyes simultaneously, and with the same thought. He said, "Will you marry me?" and before the words were out of his mouth, she said "Yes."

"Go on," John Parks was saying.

Sophie shook her head.

"Sorry," he said, handing her a tissue. "I've upset you."

"Not at all." She dabbed her eyes, her nose. "I've just realised ..."

"Go on, treat yourself," he said, *"Blow."*

She laughed, and gave her nose a proper blow. "I'm actually fine," she explained.

He squeezed her arm. "Good. Anyway, you look cute when you cry."

"Oh, thankyou," she said. "Thankyou."

"I'm just going for a smoke."

"A smoke? You devil! You didn't mention that on your profile."

He gave her a look: *There's a lot you don't know about me*, grabbed his jacket and made for the door.

Alone in the booth, she thought of what she'd explain to him when he returned: She'd been so busy hating Andy she'd forgotten that she'd ever loved him. She'd convinced herself that love was a delusion. But of *course* it was real. And that was wonderful news! Because if she could love once, she could do so again. John's drink was finished, she saw, and so finished hers too, slipping into her jacket, ready to get out of the bar and back to his place as soon as he returned to the table.

The lights had dimmed further, the music was louder and more clubby, and the place was filling up by the time she decided she'd better look for John Parks. She stood up and her head swam. He was not among the smokers clustered around the heaters and outdoor tables. She pushed her way through the bar but he wasn't there either. She phoned him and got no answer. Everyone in the bar seemed to know each other and to be having such intense conversations. She stood in the middle of the room, gazing around like an invisible ghost.

Sophie let herself in and kicked off her shoes. On the kitchen table was a pack of children's socks. Sophie grabbed a pen and paper, scrawled a note: "Thanks for everything, Mum. Love Soph xxxxxx."

Her back throbbed as she climbed the stairs. She paused outside the spare room, hearing in her mother's snoring a low murmur of grief. She went into Nell's room, sat by the cot, listening to her breathing. Then she lifted her daughter out. A thin beam of moonlight illuminated the sleeping child's face. Sophie buried her nose in her hair, kissed her soft forehead. Nell began to stir. Sophie laid her back in the cot and went to her room.

She turned off her phone and chucked it into a dark corner. Without removing her dress, she slipped under the covers and closed her eyes. She had loved once, she could still love, and she would be loved again. But now she had to get as much sleep as possible, so that tomorrow she could focus on what mattered most – caring for her daughter, raising her with exemplary strength and courage, so that one day she could become a strong, independent woman, capable of finding love and lasting joy.

The Men in Yellow Overalls

After my diagnosis and the inevitable panic, Grace and I were able to discuss the options calmly, and we decided to avail ourselves of the new laws.

Grace is affectionate as well as sensible, and she managed to commit to the decision without ever making me feel that she wouldn't miss me terribly. I felt blessed to have her. She's small, Grace, even smaller than me, but she's strong and pretty and her lovely blue eyes are undimmed by age.

Once we'd got all the paperwork sorted there was no point in not getting on with it, especially as the pain was starting to get pretty crummy. So one Monday morning I put on a good suit and she drove us to the local post office.

There was a long queue and it was stuffy and smelly in there. I think it was this that made me feel light-headed, but Grace got concerned and asked if I was having second thoughts. I smiled and shook my head, squeezing her hand.

I handed my papers to the girl on the counter.

"I'm afraid we can't provide that service at the moment, sir."

"What? That's disgraceful!" I said. Grace nudged me so I said in a more polite tone, "What appears to be the problem?"

"I'm afraid the electric chair has – well, it's run out of electricity."

"Eh? Can't you just plug it in? Change its battery?"

"Sorry. A man's coming to fix it but he won't be here until next month. January's always a busy time. Have you considered going private?"

She printed off an address, I programmed it into the Sat Nav and off we set.

"We should have brought a picnic," said Grace when she realised it was an hour's drive to a village in the Yorkshire Dales.

We arrived at the Gilbert's Guillotines and parked by a sombre-looking sign with off-white writing on a brown background, and an image of a guillotine. This seemed to get to Grace and she blinked back tears.

"Please don't cry. Look, I'm just so glad I finally found someone worth loving. Come on."

But wouldn't you know it? The lad at reception sucked his teeth, shaking his head.

"... I mean, it *sort* of works, but it comes down a bit too slowly and – well, it's not worth the risk. We've ordered a new one. It'll be here a week on Tuesday. No? I can give you the address of somewhere else that might be able to help. Their methods aren't quite what we have here, but it's cheaper."

We found the abattoir at the end of a long, winding track and parked in the Disabled bay. Grace held my hand as we approached.

Cattle were being herded into an austere-looking stone building. We heard the echoing of their lowing and their screams. A foreman emerged to greet us, smiling in his blood-spattered yellow overalls. He showed us into a cramped office.

"So no luck at guillotine place?" He rolled his

eyes. "Got your papers? Excellent."

He handed me a form. "Just read that and sign."

It was set out like a comic strip. In square one the male figure stood while a faceless assistant bound his legs together. In the second he was hanging upside down, looking stoical, like Kirk Douglas in *Spartacus*. In the third a blade had appeared and was slitting his throat, producing an improbably meagre amount of blood. The fourth showed him lying at peace, a pretty, black-clad widow placing a bunch of flowers on his chest.

I looked at Grace and she nodded. I signed.

The foreman walked ahead with his head bowed, respecting our need to have a moment together.

"You've been a wonderful husband, Jim. And you're doing the right thing."

"I wouldn't want to put you through - "

"I know. You're kind. You always were. I just wish I'd met you sooner, so we'd have had more time."

"Better late than never."

She hugged me and then kissed me quite fiercely.

Inside the cattle were queuing at a turnstile. Most of them just looked grumpy, but the odd one – the clever ones, I suppose – looked nervous. One in particular seemed to twig what was going on and started bucking about in the queue, making a horrible screaming noise, not a noise you'd think a cow could make at all. But a couple of staff in the yellow overalls stabbed him in the rump with a tranquillising syringe, got him back in the queue and into the next room.

In there it was harshly bright. I looked away as the ones ahead of me had their turn. But I could hear what was happening, obviously. It had a rhythm to it: scream of panic and incomprehension, gurgle, splash. Well, *I* wouldn't scream. By the time I stepped up to position the floor was slick with blood. But then a bored-looking lad in a baseball cap hosed it down. Drops of cold water splashed through my socks. I should have worn wellies.

Another yellow-overalls chap appeared and gestured for me to put my legs together. As he bound my ankles I looked up and saw that I was next to a window. Out of it I could see Grace. She had her winter hat on and she was waving at me like a child, clasping and unclasping her hand. With her other hand she held a tissue to her face and dabbed her pretty blue eyes. Then the rope tightened, I breathed in and Grace's eyes were blocked off suddenly by the backs of her black-gloved hands.

Remain

When I thought of dumping my boyfriend I pictured:

Having more time to devote to the Party, going on lots of dates, finding a man who didn't send flirty emails to a colleague called *Suzy*. Someone who at least attempted DIY and had more ... *ambition*. Someone sexy, powerful, well off. Does this make me a hypocrite? Probably. Actually, yes.

Election campaigns always do something weird to me. It's easy to forget that the feelings they inspire don't last forever. I was away a lot. I was running off adrenaline, bonding with my fellow soldiers in a war we were going to win. And Martin, with his complaints about his boss, his Saturday football matches and Sunday lunches with his mum, seemed like a phase I'd outgrown. And then, with three weeks to go to election day, when I discovered he'd been emailing *Suzy* again ... I made more of a fuss about it than was necessary, I suppose. When he said that nothing had Happened, I believed him. He has an almost neurotic reluctance to lie (one reason he'd never last in politics). But still I had a point, didn't I, that he must have been *thinking* about something Happening? Then he broke down and actually, like, *cried* and did that speech about how lonely he'd been while I was away. A more decent person might have melted at that. But I'd gone too far in picturing life without him, and I got sort of ... drunk on power, I guess. Before I knew it I was saying the terrible, exhilarating words I'd half-planned on saying for weeks. I didn't expect him to give up so quickly. One minute we were sitting at the table, unable to face that chicken casserole he'd made, having that tearful conversation; the next he was packing.

"Why should I waste a moment longer," he said, chucking stuff into a suitcase I'd not seen since our holiday in Morocco two years ago, "with someone who doesn't love me?"

93

"Of course I *love* you. It's just that ..."

He gave me a moment to finish and, when I didn't, pushed past me to the door.

It was very quiet after he left. The sort of silence that lurks around you, gathering force in the corners of the room. So, yes I went and found the Emergency Cigarettes. I sat back at the table, using the casserole dish as an ashtray, planning my political career and telling myself I'd just done a brutal but necessary thing.

Over the coming days the silence was easily filled. There was no time for a long, dark night of the soul. As well as running the regional press office, I was effectively joint-managing the local campaign. I was on my phone all night until I fell asleep, then the alarm would go off and I'd get that surge of adrenaline that would propel me out of bed and back onto the campaign trail. To win, you have to see yourself winning. You have to visualise. And boy, was I visualising. Geoffrey, whose seat we were defending, was dropping hints about how there might be a better job for me after the election. A London job. A *Westminster* job. I pictured myself as an MP. Then a cabinet post. Home Secretary, maybe, and who knows? One day, even ... Look, I *know*, right?

I didn't picture:
Losing the election, obviously.

I didn't picture the pay cut and counting the coppers and having to drop the gym membership and the subscription to the *New Statesman*. I didn't picture the overnight massacre of jobs, coming into the office and finding there was just me, for hours on end, with not all that much to do. Then home to the empty flat where I'd fuck about on Twitter, trying not to smoke.

Summer faded; the bed grew cold. But getting to sleep wasn't the half of it. Staying there was the challenge. I began to have a regular nightmare, which I came to think of as The Noise. I'm confronted by a disapproving auntie type in a blue dress (a Tory auntie, naturally), frowning at her watch, turkey wattle wobbling as she shakes head in disapproval tinged with schadenfreude. Then she looks at me. I try to shout at her but she puts a choking hand around my throat. Then she opens her mouth, but instead of words out of her mouth comes this hideous clicking sound: *tick-tick-tick-tick-tick.*

I felt sorry for myself. I felt sorry for all of us. I had a bit of a cry when I was helping Geoffrey out of the office with his cardboard boxes. And I felt *really* sorry for Ed. You could tell he was as shocked as anyone. Before he left for Ibiza, I found myself in Doncaster, on my way back from a profoundly depressing strategy meeting. I had an hour to kill, changing trains, and I stopped to use the loo in this little café. They were putting up the chairs, sweeping the floor, and at a table in the corner there was Ed, miserably munching a panini. There were two blokes with him, fiddling with their phones. No one was talking. I could have introduced myself of course, commiserated. I've met him a few times and he's always remembered me and been lovely. But I didn't think he'd appreciate the interruption. Ed was struggling with the Mozzarella in his sandwich – you know how you can get strings of the stuff that just go on and on? And I looked at him, this man who we thought was going to be Prime Minister, whose legacy would be a more compassionate capitalism, making these clumsy little loops with his fork while his aides looked down at their phones and I thought: Mate, if it wasn't for Justine, you'd be fucked.

But you fight on. My dad taught me that. He spent decades pounding the streets, taking shit on the doorstep. Three years before his first heart attack he got one lousy term on the council before losing to the fucking BNP. Still he kept on. You have to believe or you're nothing. The point is, it wasn't enough for me to send out the odd press release. I had to get back to the grass roots, hear the arguments, even allow myself to be persuaded of the virtues of this crusty old Trot called Jeremy Corbyn. Anything to drown out The Noise.

The far left had been around forever, of course. But if you came of age during the Blair years, as I did, they'd never seemed like a serious threat. They were dinosaurs. Then suddenly we were up to our *arses* in dinosaurs – in freshly hatched velociraptors snapping their bright young teeth and screeching *Blairite!* and *Red Tory!*

The meeting billed as What Next for Labour? It was in a community hall opposite that awful high-rise university hall of residence, and was hosted by Susan Leatherman. Remember her, Martin? She came to my thirtieth, which admittedly is a while ago now. You couldn't ask for a more dedicated constituency MP. She never got from Tony the attention she felt was her due but she didn't let that bias her against him. She's strong, principled. I spoke to her on the phone after election day and she was admirably tough about it all, having just held onto her seat. We'd be back, she said. You had to take the long view. Europe would do for Cameron's government like it had for all the others. Time, she soothed, was on our side.

I arrived early just as she was testing the mic. She stepped off the stage, gave me a hug and held me by the arms.

"Now. Are you alright, Laura?"

For a moment I thought she must have heard about Martin leaving. But then I realised she meant, did I still have a job?

"Yes. They've kept me on at the press office."

She smiled. "Everyone values the work you do. That's what I've been hearing."

No idea, looking back, how true that was. But you can imagine how much I wanted to believe her.

I sat near the front. The room began to fill. There were lots of them and most of them were young, which I took to be good signs. But then Sue started speaking and I realised something was wrong. She was trying to buck us up with talk of our achievements. The minimum wage, protection of worker's rights, action on child poverty. Then someone said, *"Illegal war!"*

Sue's a pro, and she barely paused. But a moment later there was hissing, as if the pantomime villain had walked on stage in a green fog of dry ice.

"Blairite!" someone said, smothered in a cough. Then there was some pretend sneezing and Sue stopped talking and glared, which made them laugh all the more.

Suddenly I was back at school again, feeling sorry for the supply teacher.

"Not to mention," said Sue, leaning into the microphone, "Our proud history of confronting racism. *Including anti-Semitism.*"

There were sniggers and someone said, "I've just got a cold! *A – Jew!*" and that did it. I was on my feet turning round.

"Pack it in!"

The laughter died away.

"You should be ashamed of yourselves!"

Martin always said I'm scary when I'm angry. Well, that has its uses. It went quiet. I was staring at row upon row of handsomely bearded hipsters; young women, faces tight with moral conviction; a clutch of Asian men and their implacably veiled wives. The girl behind me, insolently chewing gum, was pointing a phone at me, filming it all. The familiar faces in the crowd looked old, frightened, outnumbered.

I sat down. Sue gave me a discreet nod, continued speaking. For a while there was no more heckling, and I began to feel proud of myself. But then Sue turned a page in her speech and I knew she was coming up to a passage praising Tony, and she was about to change her mind, but then thought, *no, that's giving in to them*, so went ahead with it anyway. But she rushed it, trying to get it over with as the hissing started up again, along with more of that '*a-Jew*' shit.

Then she was off the stage and it was the next speaker's turn, a white Muslim woman called Safa Haque, who I recognised as a former grammar school teacher called Kath Blunt. She did a Tory-bashing posh-boy-scum routine. She tore into Trident, using the old penis-extension analogy. She made a joke, if you could call it that, about Cameron and the pig's head. She *raised the roof* with a line about how the Tories' secret plan was to shaft the NHS to the point of *having* to privatise it. She attacked the 'lies' of the 'Zionist lobby' and the 'mainstream media'. Oh, they fucking loved her, Martin. You'd have puked.

Afterwards there was a mass exodus to the pub across the street. I went behind the stage, looking for Sue. But she must have already left and who could blame her?

I stepped outside for an Emergency Cigarette. Smoking outside already was a handsome bloke with a shaved head and kind eyes.

"Good night?"

"I've had better."

He smiled.

"How was yours?"

"Oh, I'm just the caretaker, love. It's all the same to me. But I was watching. I'm Gareth."

I shook his proffered hand, felt its rough palm. "You were pretty feisty in there," he said.

I bristled, hearing something annoyingly gender-specific in 'feisty'. But he meant it as a compliment. "Thanks. It wasn't enough, though, was it?"

He shrugged. "You tried." He was gorgeous, I noticed. Sort of tough but soulful-looking with long-lashed eyes. Too young for me, though.

"Night, Gareth."

"Don't go yet."

I hesitated. Was he going to invite me out? I looked into his eyes and before I could stop myself imagined them gazing into mine across a pillow.

"Why not?" I said, raising an eyebrow, quite the coquette.

He looked down, grinding out his cigarette with his toe. "Because you've got chewing gum in your hair."

I wanted to get straight off then, but he wouldn't let me. He took me into the dressing-room, which had a mirror, and from a tool kit produced a pair of scissors. He stood behind me, put those hands on my shoulders. We locked eyes in the mirror and it was all I could do not to press my arse into him. God, I'd been so fucking lonely.

Then he shook his head as if to clear it, began making little cuts with the scissors. "So where's your husband tonight?"

I sighed. "You know, I'd have preferred it if you'd said 'boyfriend'."

"Ah. You'd have felt younger."

"No husband," I said. "No boyfriend either."

He caught my eye and this time I had to look away.

"You realise it's over, don't you?" he said.

"What?"

"The Labour Party." He shifted my hair, made a more decisive cut. "The centre-left in general."

"Bollocks," I said.

"Maybe." He plucked out the gob of gum, turned it over in his palm, tossed it into the bin. He smiled at me in the mirror. "Fancy a pint?" he said.

We walked up the road, avoiding the velociraptors at the big, studenty place nearby. We carried our pints to a cosy booth.

It turned out that he only volunteered at the church hall. He was actually a plumber. He watched me as he revealed this, checking my reaction, which was … Ooooh, mixed. You know: Look at good little lefty me, having a beer with a genuine, honest-to-God member of the working class. Also a faint pang of intellectual snobbery and squeamishness: *All that shitty water!* I'm not proud of either reaction, by the way.

I asked him about being a plumber and he told me about it. But there was a bit of irony in his delivery now. He intensified his Yorkshire accent on words like 'monkey-wrench' and 'effluence', as if satirising the class difference between us.

"Oh," I said at one point, distracted by the proximity of his large, dark eyes and manfully gesturing hands. "That's interesting."

He laughed. "Is it bollocks, Laura. But it pays the bills."

I liked the sound of my name on his tongue. I asked if it was true that indigenous plumbers were being forced out of work by a flood of immigrants.

"Not round here. We have one of the lowest levels of immigration in the country, as you probably know. But that didn't stop half the people I know voting UKIP. But come on, if Polish plumbers are getting hired, it's because they're good. The answer is to make sure you're better. That's capitalism, mate."

"You didn't vote UKIP, then."

"Don't tell the lads. It's bad enough that I make them listen to Radio Four when we're on the job. I prefer the *Today* programme to Chris Evans? I *must* be a poof."

My head was spinning with challenged prejudices and sexual fantasies. I managed to get out, "So how did you vote?"

"Tory, mate."

And the curious thing was, I did not feel an almost physical repulsion, did not enjoy the hot spurt of righteous anger at being confronted with a morally inferior specimen. I did, however, feel the dark-chocolatey thrill of transgression. I know: What was wrong with me? Blame the velociraptors.

Gareth was chuckling. "Oh dear. Your face, Laura. You fucking hate me now, don't you?" He didn't seem particularly bothered about this.

"I don't actually. Don't tell *my* mates. So. Why Tory?"

"I *wanted* to vote for Miliband. But, come on, really? Sorry, he's probably a friend of yours and I'm sure he means well, but … In times like this you need a government that can take the harsh decisions to get you through a rough patch. It's not a time for pissing about, virtue-signalling. I think Cameron's made a serious mistake, though."

"Really? And what's that?"

"The referendum. He'll lose."

"Bollocks," I said. "You need to get out more."

He shrugged. I liked the way he was happy to disagree. I don't get that much from people. "Maybe." He drained his pint. "One for the road?"

When he returned with the next round he was in a playful mood. He began challenging me to name the shadow cabinet.

"You're competitive, aren't you?"

"You ain't seen nothing yet," he said, producing a pen and paper.

He turned the whole thing into a game, kept score, though the rules were vague. Before I knew it we were arm-wrestling, collapsing into giggles.

We held hands in the back of the cab and by the time it pulled up outside his flat we were kissing.

He wanted to carry me up the stairs.

"Show-off!"

"Come on." He held out his arms for me to fall into.

"I'm too feminist for that nonsense."

"Alright, compromise. Piggy back."

I jumped onto his back and he made a pantomime of being surprised at how heavy I was, so I could spitefully kick him in the thighs with my high heels. He took me up two flights of stairs and we collapsed, laughing onto his bed.

The first time he was all panting, thrusting and flexing muscles. I thought: typical twenty-something man raised on internet porn. But the second time he was gentle and patient, rocking me slowly, like he had all the time in the world, into orgasm. Did he enjoy this variety? Or was it more that he was proving a point, that he had more than one tool in his kit, so to speak? I stopped wondering about this and fell asleep with his rough-palmed hand stroking my hair.

So yes, Martin. It Happened. He applied his spanner to my nuts and bolts. He unblocked my clogged-up pipes. He stuck his plunger deep into my u-bend. Seriously though. It reminded me what I'd been missing. *We* used to have that. Where did it go? You move in together, you let it slide. Because there's always tomorrow night, isn't there? Until suddenly there isn't.

I woke up late, in a panic. On the way out of his flat I stubbed my toe on his tool box. The ache in my foot that day seemed of a piece with the other bits of me that were sore, sweetly painful reminders of what a great time I'd had.

The morning was slow, and I had a lot of time to make myself cups of tea and remember my night with the gorgeous plumber. But then the calls started, first from the local papers, then the nationals What exactly had happened at last night's meeting? I was deliberately vague with some haughty cow from the *Telegraph*.

"Come on, Laura," she said. "You can do better than this. I'm reliably informed that you were there. So: Were there or were there not anti-Semitic comments made during Susan Leatherman's speech?"

I told her I'd have to call her back.

"Twenty minutes," she said and hung up.

Fuming, I tried to raise Susan Leatherman, couldn't get through, ended up having to cobble together some crap about 'disruption' and 'reports of anti-Semitic comments'. I was *not* going to describe for the Tory-graph the exact nature of the racist sneezing. I finished off my statement with something about how Labour did not tolerate anti-Semitism. When it came back from central office, they'd added "*... or other forms of racism*," which to me looked shifty, but there was no time to argue, so I had to send it as it was, and felt grubby and compromised for the rest of the day.

Who had leaked what happened to the press? Not the velociraptors, surely? Someone on my side, trying to discredit them? What *was* my side exactly? Oh, shit, I could see where this was going.

I was tempted to call Gareth, but even I know that's not the done thing now. So I waited two days before sending him a message. I wanted to be witty, so looked up the members of the cabinet from a few years ago, then texted him. 'Who's Margaret Becket? You're not allowed to look her up, obvs."

A couple of hours later I started to regret this. Maybe that tone belonged to our pre-shag selves, and now I was failing to appreciate the transforming nature of the sex we'd had. So I tried again.

"I miss you. Can we meet next weekend?"

Then I spent a few days anxiously checking my phone for messages, imagining hearing it ring, even grabbing it out of my bag to find that it was mute.

I was anxiously watching *Question Time*, drinking cheap Merlot and smoking my way through a pack of Emergency Cigarettes when his text finally arrived.

'That was a nice night but I'm afraid I'm a bit busy also loved up with a new bird sorry. PS: Margaret Beckett (two t's) is Labour. Foreign secretary and then housing minister. Led the No to AV campaign. Survived the expenses scandal. Now something on a select committee? Take care.'

"Fucking Tories," I said aloud.

I thought that was quite a cool reaction. But there was no-one there to hear it.

There were other blokes, but there's not much of the winter of 2015 to '16 that I care to remember. Only when the referendum campaign kicked in did the gloom begin to lift. Here was another battle to be fought, and one we were pretty much guaranteed to win.

But oh my God.

They sent me to Doncaster, where again and again I found myself arguing on the doorsteps of Brexiteers. Would Britain be better off leaving the EU? They didn't seem to be hearing that question at all. For many of them, it was, Is your life a bit shit? And since the answer was yes, they were voting leave. It was crazy, of course. But then who was I to talk? I can't pretend to be totally baffled by the appeal of a self-inflicted wound in the name of independence. *Take back control!* Is that what I'd thought I was doing?

You know when people talk about 'shouting at the TV'? It's usually done as a bit of a laugh. But there was nothing funny about it when I found myself shouting at the TV late on June 23. There were people in that room more exhausted than I was, who had known Jo Cox much better than I did, and when I think of them I still burn with shame.

We were watching Nigel Farage on the big TV mounted on the wall. He was celebrating the victory for 'real', 'ordinary', and 'decent' people.

"And we will have done it without having to fight," he was saying, his head snapping back and forth, "Without a single bullet being fired -"

"A bullet *was* fired, you fucking idiot!"

I can't remember what else I shouted. It was Susan Leatherman who bundled me out. She gave me a hug and brought me some sugary tea. Without explicitly saying so she made it clear that I wasn't allowed back in until I'd got my shit together.

Nine o'clock, June 24. I was removing the Remain banner from outside the house when Martin walked up the drive. He wore a nice fitting suit with his tie askew. Without saying anything he hugged me. A chaste hug, but still it felt good. He looked at me and laughed, but sympathetically.

"Glass of wine?"

"Why? So you can hear all about my failures?"

"No. Just thought you might fancy a chat."

Now he looked hurt, I realised I didn't really want to hurt him. He turned and began walking back to his car.

"Wait, Martin."

He turned round.

"Stay."

"You sure?"

"Yes. Stay." I held up the poster: *Remain.*

In the pub he explained that he lived only a few streets away. He'd moved out of his mum's and was renting a 'shitty flat above a shop'.

But he looked good. His hair was longer in a way that disguised the recession at his temples, and from the way his bicep flexed as he poured the wine I could tell he'd maintained the gym habit.

"So how are you?"

"How are *you*?" he said. His tone implied that I was the one we needed to worry about. We talked about the election, about Corbyn, about the referendum result,

114

about Hilary and Trump, but before I knew it I was spilling my guts about the plumber.

"He sounds alright. Still seeing him?"

"Nah. It was just a bit of fun."

He looked at me. "Really?"

He always understood me. Even when I was bullshitting him.

But then he was standing up, answering his phone. "Hi, Suzy," he said as he stepped away from the table.

He took the call at the far end of the room. I went out for an Emergency Cigarette. When I returned he was back at the table. And if he smelt the tobacco on me he didn't mention it.

"So," I said. "*Suzy*. How long's that been going on for?"

"It hasn't."

"Bollocks."

"Last month I was made regional manager. I've been transferred to the Leeds office. We went for a meal last week and ... it wasn't the same."

"Why not? She was gagging for it, Martin. And you were -"

"Well - I think it was all based on being in the same office together, being at the same level. But now she takes liberties because we used to be mates and she thinks she can get away with it, and I'm in this awkward position where I have to phone her up and give her a bollocking. So I told her just now that I couldn't see her tonight because I was with you. She didn't like that."

"So you haven't even shagged her?"

"Nope. Turned out I didn't want to."

I topped up my glass and drank, surprised at how relieved I felt.

"So. Regional manager, eh? Bit of a pay rise?"

He met my eye as he revealed the figure.

"Wow." I felt him watching me, in spite of myself, making calculations. "Congratulations."

"Since you kicked me out I realised that weekends are just empty when you're single unless you actively fill them. And all my mates are in couples now. So I started going into the office on Saturdays and putting together a sort of overview of the whole company. I presented it to my boss along with some suggestions. He was impressed. So when a vacancy came up, I thought I might as well go for it. I should be able to rent somewhere better before long."

"Of course."

"I don't think I'll get my deposit back. I'd been thinking about what you said about DIY. So I tried putting up a towel rail on the bathroom door. Now it looks like someone's been at it with a machine gun."

"Maybe DIY is not for you."

"Maybe." His smile faded. "Does it make a difference to how you feel about me?"

"The towel rail?"

"The money."

He was trying to look casual but I noticed his hand was tight on his wine glass and the muscle in his jaw was clenching.

"Would you think less of me if it did?"

"Not sure I *could* think less of you, to be honest, Laura."

"Oh, thanks!"

"I just mean that I think I know you now. I know the real Laura." He let out a helpless chuckle that crinkled the corners of his eyes. "And still I miss her."

"It's not just the money. It's like you were barely even trying. When I was working so hard."

"Well, maybe I've learnt something. So. How's the single life?"

"Oh, it's great. It's humbling. I've been having nightmares." I told him about The Noise. "It's such a cliché."

"There's nothing wrong with being worried about running out of time. Fertility drops sharply in women after -"

"Yeah, yeah. Thanks, Martin."

"Look, I worry about it too."

"It's not the same for men."

"No. But." He put a palm to the side of my face, making me look at him. "It's not that different either."

The hand on my face seemed to do something to him and he sat back. "Sorry." He drank the rest of his wine, tried to smile. "I know you'll never give up the fight. I love that about you. But you are allowed to take a break for – for other things. Look at it this way, Laura. Do you really want to be alone that morning in November when you wake up and Donald Trump is the next president?"

"God, don't even joke about it."

I reached for his hand.

The waiter came over. Martin nodded to the empty bottle. "Shall we get another?"

"Let's take one home."

"Home? Where's that?"

Later I was lying on the bed while he straddled my hips and looked down on me. The setting sun cast a gleam of warm light over his body, but his face was in shadow. Then he leaned down and kissed me. There was aggression in the kiss and for a moment I almost felt scared. What if he wanted revenge?

He straightened, breathing hard. "Are you using anything?"

"No, but there are some jonnies in the drawer."

He put his hands on either side of my face and said softly, "Let's not bother with contraception."

"What? Are you kidding? Why?"

"Oh, Laura ..." His hands seemed to tremble. He bent over me and kissed me again, more gently this time. He smoothed my hair against my cheek. His lips moved to my ear. "Tick tick tick," he said.

Spice World

"Okay, so in what *order* would you shag the Spice Girls?"

We're round at Tommo's. It's the school holidays, his parents are in France and we're drinking Special Brew, smoking roll-ups and watching *Top of the Pops*. We are all virgins.

"Say you had one night with all of them. What order?"

My little brother takes a drag, winces. "I'd start with Mel C. I wouldn't mind a bit of zig-a-zig-ah with *her*."

"What?" I lean into him, gratified by the nervous look in his eyes. "She's *hideous!*"

He blushes. "Alright, then. Geri."

"Nice tits," says Tommo.

"Fat slag," I say on a plume of scorching smoke.

***

I'm in a beer garden with my little brother. I've been trying to get him to talk about his divorce but he's distracted by his three-year-old venturing onto the climbing frame. The sun is burning my bald spot and neither of us has brought a hat. I delve into my bag, looking for sun lotion, but I find instead the Spice Girls CD I bought at a jumble sale that morning. I bought it, ostensibly, for my own daughter, who sits beside me eating fish fingers.

"Okay," I say, placing the CD on the table in front of my brother. "In what order would you S - H - A - G them?"

I can't read his expression behind his shades. Is he remembering how I used to belittle him in front of Tommo? But then he says, "You mean now, or in – what? 1996?"

"Ninety-six. At the time, I'd have said: Ginger, Baby, Posh, Scary, Sporty. That's the order of how S - H - A - G -able I found them. But it doesn't seem so simple now I'm older. *Now*, I'd start with -"

My brother gets up to tend to his little girl, who

has slipped off the climbing frame and is screaming for him. So I don't get to tell him that I doubt I could manage all five Spice Girls in one night. So I'd start not with my favourite, but with my *least* favourite, Sporty, while I was still full of spunk. Then I'd square up to the intimidating lariness, the exotic blackness of Scary; after which I'd brace myself for the footballer's wife, whose insolent gaze I'd long to see soften in the throes of orgasm. But what if I failed? Which, let's face it, I probably would? I'd slip out of her, open my eyes to face that dreaded pout of discontent ... But then to the rescue would bounce the voluptuous treat of Ginger. If anyone could find juice in me now, *she* could. Her air of experience, relative age and yes, generous curves would be sweet succour after the grating humiliation of Posh. Then, at sunrise, exhaustion starting to blur my vision and shake my limbs, I'd be summoned by the soft voice and forgiving, blue eyes of Baby. Ah, yes. On I'd wade, more in hope than expectation, into the coolly soothing waters of Bunton ...

***

I wake at 4am. I remember that my ex-wife, daughter and brother have all chosen to live far away. Like a hangover from a dream of youth, *Wannabe* by the Spice Girls canters through my head. To soothe myself back to sleep I ask the old question.

These days, one would be enough, and I'd choose Sporty, Mel C, *Melanie Chisholm*, who was anything but 'hideous'. How could I have overlooked, even at 14, everything in that face that was loveable?

I imagine us on holiday. Nothing flash. A guest house in the Lakes, perhaps. Our kids are at university now and we enjoy gentle walks – or rather drives, what with my dodgy hip – in the country. In a comfortable hotel room I massage moisturiser into her shoulders, kneading the well-padded slope of her back and the cushion of her buttocks.

"Ah, that's nice, love," she says in that sing-song Scouse accent. She sighs, then surprises me by reaching a hand around her back and taking my cock. She plays with it for a bit, then slips it inside. She looks at me over her shoulder and her face crinkles in a playful smile.

"Zig-a-zig-ah," she says.

Walking Shadow

1.

The exposure of my role in what was later known as the Prentice case began in the spring term of 2003. I opened the door of my office at the faculty of Media, Critical and Creative Arts to two police officers.

I had, of course, been expecting the police. But there was something about the way they looked at me – the bloke in particular – that betrayed a certain excitement. Was I a potential suspect?

"Of course," I said. "Come in. I'd offer you a seat, but as you can see …"

It's small, my office. Sometimes that's been to my advantage, I think. But not today. I could smell the fish and chips they'd had for lunch. The strained shirt buttons of the bloke were inches from my face, even though he tried to sort of slouch against my book case.

"Actually," said the woman, "We were hoping

you'd come with us."

***

Simon Prentice: Before I laid eyes on him, I'd heard the name in the faculty canteen, in tones of exasperation, but also affection. We could be pretty brutal about the ones we didn't like. It's a way of letting off steam, I suppose. And we're lonely. We spend too long reading, writing, starting at screens, lying awake at night haunted by young, questioning faces. Racing to stay ahead of the bright, fretting about the failures of the stupid. And many of us live in a state of perennial sexual frustration. I mean here you are, surrounded by hundreds of young women, many of them hanging on your every word and hungry for experience. And you have to act like you don't have a cock. It's exhausting. Anyway, I wanted to make the point that we talked about the students, and I'd heard of Prentice before I met him. I suppose if my overheard impressions added up to anything it was of someone eccentric, demanding, admirably yet comically serious, one of the few remaining *earnest* young people, someone quite out of step, you might say, with the mood of his generation.

So when I got the class list for one of my seminar groups on *Macbeth*, I recognised his name before I was able to put it with the slim, rather formally dressed young man in the front row. We read some *Macbeth*. And to be honest I didn't think that he was all that bright, because he ... he just couldn't get *over* Macbeth. I mean, he couldn't *stand* that motherfucker. Yes, I'm afraid Prentice was labouring, or so I thought, under that tediously reductive notion that we should *like the characters*. What did he think this was? *A Good Read* with Sue MacGregor? His outrage, though, was genuine. He had a long neck, and the arteries in it were bulging as he made his protests. I listened to him, but I watched the girls. I usually do watch the girls, because on the whole I find them more interesting. I thought the gothy one called Claire was quite impressed by his ardour, whereas the gorgeous, glossy Sabrina had a look of almost physical disgust creasing the corners of her well powdered nose. She didn't do ardour. You could tell.

Then the older girl - the mature one whom I later found out was three years older than me and had an unforgettable birthmark, like a third nipple, between her breasts - she smiled indulgently, clearly enjoying herself, a bright, bored woman who was profoundly grateful to be in the company of a boy whose arteries bulged as he attacked Macbeth. A change, I imagined, from singing *The Wheels On The Bus* for the thirtieth time, bouncing an infant on her knee, semi-dreading the return of her remote, distracted, stressed-out, paunchy, irascible husband. My God, you wouldn't believe (or perhaps you would) the reservoirs of boredom and loneliness one encounters in some of these women, the vast planes of unharvested lust, the stuffed vaults of unplundered loot …

Prentice reminded me of my younger self. He demanded a challenge to what he'd said, but spoilt everyone's appetite for debate by going in too hot. I filled the silence.

"I don't disagree with anything you've said. But nor would Macbeth. And that's what makes him interesting. He *knows* he's doing the wrong thing, but does it anyway."

I loved what happened next. Prentice started to object but then gave up and said, "You know, I think that's what annoyed me so much. I'm ashamed of myself for identifying with him."

A couple of the girls glanced at each other. Not the older bird, though. No, *she* actually reached across and patted Prentice's hand. As she withdrew she glanced at me and gave a maternal cringe of affection that creased her chin. *Isn't he sweet?* She had soft brown eyes and a thick blonde bob. Her body was all soft curves but her nails were painted bright blue and looked very sharp. I imagined them scoring down my back. I twinkled my eyes at her before we moved on and Prentice became secondary to the rest of that morning's seminar as I schemed ways to get this woman to the pub at lunch time.

We had six pints from 1 to 5pm, then went back to hers. Jo, she was called. I wanted to call her Josephine but she wouldn't let me. She had a lovely mouth. What I kept thinking about though, apart from the mouth and the birth mark, is the way she stroked Prentice's knee when he got all emotional about Macbeth. I must be getting old. I *am* getting old. Another thing: the condom was leaking when I withdrew. Perhaps she'd snagged it with her sharp nails. I didn't mention it, but I remembered.

2.

Then Prentice handed in an essay and I started to respect him a bit more. It was well researched and had that combination of emotional engagement and objectivity that you hope for. There was a handwritten note at the end, which said he'd become interested in murder and conscience and wanted to do his dissertation on it, starting with *Macbeth*. I marked the essay, adding a recommendation that he read *Crime and Punishment.* But I had a vague misgiving. Wouldn't Prentice be more comfortable - more psychologically *safe* - with, say, a commentary on the changing nature of stage management from the Elizabethan period to the early 21st century?

I should really have marked some more essays, but it was Friday night and the session with Josephine had left me so exhausted that even several days later I'd not quite recovered. I was thinking: curry, bottle of wine, video. Something American, violent, undemanding. Directly across the road from my office was the union bar, which had begun to warm up for its big event: Beats Against Bush. Yes, the university ents people had organised a disco, club-night, whatever, in protest against the invasion. I know - the silence from the White House was deafening. But here, *Born Slippy* was thumping out so loud that even across the road I could feel the throb of the bass. I was slightly tempted to *go* to Beats Against Bush. I could get into some amusing arguments with some of the students. But who's to say they weren't right about Iraq? No, I needed that early night. So I wasn't thrilled when, just as I was locking my door, I heard a voice say, "Thank God I caught you," and turned to see Prentice hurrying towards me down the dimly lit corridor.

"Have you got a minute?"

"Aren't you going to Beats Against Bush?"

He looked out of the window at the union bar.

"I keep thinking about you day."

That's what it sounded like he said. I stifled a yawn. Perhaps he was nuts after all.

"I could see you tomorrow," I said. "I mean Monday." Boy, was I knackered.

He looked at me. One of his eyes was bloodshot; his nose, I noticed, was wide and almost equine. He was handsome in an off-beat sort of way.

"You day," he said again.

"I'm sorry," I said, yawning openly now. "You've lost me."

"Saddam's son. Do you know much about him?"

"Ah. Uday. Yes. Tortures people for fun. Kidnaps girls and rapes them. Stuff like that. Bit of a blunt instrument, though, don't you think? Shock and awe? You don't invade Yorkshire because of Peter Sutcliffe."

"That's a bogus analogy," he said.

"Okay, well. I'm tired."

"I just can't stop thinking about him."

"Well, you should. Think about something else. I mean, look." I pointed out, through the window. "See those girls? That's where you should be, at your age. You should be bonding over your righteous indignation. Beats Against Bush might be a questionable excuse for a party, but it's still a party."

"I hate *Born Slippy*. The way they pound their fists in the air when it goes *'lager, lager, lager.'* It's about mental breakdown, that song. I read an interview with the bloke who wrote it. It's about an alcoholic depression descending into madness."

"Yeah, but it can still sound uplifting. Maybe what they're pounding their fists about is the recognition that madness is universal. Someone else feels this. Empathy is worthy of celebration. Not everything has to be a fucking funeral march, Prentice."

"But they don't understand."

"How do you know? They know they don't want the Iraq war. They know they like alcohol and sex and they respond to *Born Slippy* perhaps because they intuit its darkness. You'd feel better if you realised how much you have in common with these people. Just like you cheered up when you realised you had something in common with Macbeth. Stop holding yourself apart all the time. You're not that different."

"Yes I am."

It was getting dark in the corridor. I stepped to one side, turned on a light. Prentice blinked, but recovered quickly; his eyes were young.

"Can I just talk to you for a bit? We could go

somewhere quieter if you fancy a drink? I just feel like discussing something with someone – you know - older than me. Someone who understands stuff."

I laughed. "And what is it you imagine that I understand?"

He shrugged. "Guilt," he said. He ran a hand nervously through is hair and added, "Murder?"

I took him to the same pub as Josephine. It has quiet booths and real ale. I got us a pint each and let him talk. I started to enjoy myself. I didn't realise, you see, how serious all this would become. He went around the subject from different angles for quite a while, so I'll summarise what he said, pretty much as I did to the police that first day they took me in.

Prentice had gone out for a coffee with a group of students on his Theatre Studies module but had ended up smoking weed with them at the top of one of those awful high-rise halls on the edge of town. A very powerful spliff was passed to him by a fat, blonde girl with a pierced tongue. She nodded towards the door, from which a bloke had just exited, and huddled up to Prentice, confiding, as he pulled on the spliff. She said something like this.

"Thank God he's gone. He gives me the creeps, he really does." She was Welsh. He later worked out that her name was Holly. "He's their friend and everything but still, you know? What, you haven't heard? You don't live here, no? Oh. Right. Sorry, nothing."

Prentice got rid of the spliff, which was making him cough, and the room was starting to spin. He began to think he should leave, but wasn't ready for the ordeal of finding his way out and walking home in the dark. He thought of the streets with their groups of lads in tracksuits and baseball caps, the prostitutes by the bushes around the cathedral, his lonely, single bed. He missed his mum and his dog, and a chasm of sadness yawned beneath him. Then Holly leaned closer and said, "I keep looking at his hands and thinking of what he's done."

He looked at Holly and thought that, whatever it was, it couldn't be anything too serious, judging by the glitter of pleasure in her eyes. Maybe she was quite pretty after all.

"And what's that?"

"Well." Holly squirmed her wide bottom deeper into the bean bag she was sitting on. "When he was in sixth form, he and his mate got paid to push this old woman down the stairs. You haven't heard this, no? He took a cut of her will, which was agreed in advance, to push her down the stairs so she died. I can't look at his hands without thinking about that, that *push*. I mean I know he's good-looking. And he's very clever. I mean he's ... he's so clever. But he still gives me the creeps. I don't think Emma should be seeing him, do you? But, well, she says she loves him." She heaved a theatrical sigh, swooned, head back, ringed fingers fluttering at her cleavage. "Young love!"

What happened next was rather odd. Prentice had a very strong sense of seeing the young man who'd just left the room. He'd been sitting across from him for about an hour or so, but now he was gone, Prentice could picture him more clearly than when he was actually there. Explain that. He remembered a tall, handsome blonde boy with an athletic physique and, as he put it, 'full, sensuous lips'. He'd not been saying much, just glancing about, alert but relaxed, sceptical, unpleasantly amused. He'd been drinking a can of Carlsberg. There it was, still, slightly crumpled, on the carpet about two feet from Prentice.

The girl was running a heavily ringed hand up and down Prentice's thigh now. This caused ripples of sensation to dance up his thighs and over his arms. It was the sort of feeling that would be thrilling if he fancied the girl, but as he didn't it felt invasive and sickening. He stood up, which made him light-headed, but still he was able to find his coat and push his way out.

In the corridor, in the harsh light, there was a smell of bleach and stale cigarettes. Prentice saw a sign for the stairs and walked towards them. Then he remembered the stairs that the old woman had been pushed down. What if the bloke came back up the stairs, having forgotten his wallet or something, and detected on Prentice's face some kind of knowledge? Would he have to then throw Prentice down the stairs as well? It was horrifying that murder could happen with *stairs*. There didn't even have to be any other weapon, just a pair of treacherous arms behind you. Prentice went to the lift instead, pressed the button and waited for a very long time. When the lift door opened it did not have the bloke in. It was empty. Prentice got in, endured a minute or two of thinking he might be about to have a heart attack, dashed into the street, walked the two miles across town to the faculty of Media, Critical and Creative Arts and found me.

"Why me?" I asked when he'd finished his story.

"Why not? You said some interesting things about guilt the other day. I thought you might have a theory."

"About what? You had the misfortune to see an alleged hitman. So what - ?"

"But what should I *do* about it?"

"Nothing. Prentice, all I have to say is, don't go back there. Oh yeah, and don't smoke weed. It's poisonous. You were stoned and some girl told you some bloke had killed someone. I mean, that would do it. Go home, eat something, go to bed. Tomorrow you'll feel better."

"But he's out there. He did it and he's out there."

I felt very tired. *I* should have been in bed by now.

"There's nothing you can do about that now, is there? I mean, say you went to the police. What would they have to go on?"

"You're right. I'll forget about it. Look, will you stay with me for one more drink? I still feel a bit ..."

I glanced at my watch. Why not? I caught the waitress's eye and signalled for two more.

"I won't get you in trouble, will I? Keeping you out late?"

"No. It's fine."

"So ... Do you live by yourself?"

"Why do you ask? Yes. But most nights my girlfriend stays. After she's back from her job at the theatre. We're buying a house. Well, we might be."

"I thought Josephine was your girlfriend."

"What? Who? No. No, she's not. How do you -?"

"I saw you leaving here with her the other day.

141

You looked pretty friendly." He shook his head. Not man-to-man, simply disapproving. "You should be careful. How do you justify that, by the way?"

"Oh. Ask me another time. Tell me about your dissertation."

I made it home just before Penny arrived, and let her think I'd been there all night. I warmed up some pretty good leftover lamb bhuna. Then we slobbed in front of the telly and watched a piece of John Grisham trash called *A Time to Kill.* Penny made some comments about how gorgeous the lead actor was. And that sort of thing always makes me want to have sex with her; don't ask me why. So as soon as it was over I chased her up the stairs. I managed pretty well, considering the proximity of my afternoon with Josephine. But then, before she fell asleep, Penny did that thing where she murmurs, as if half-dreaming, "Stay with me, Al." And as usual that made me feel guilty, stifled, smothered. A further tightening of her hands around my throat.

3.

"Jesus, Al! That's a bit of a gruesome image! Love as strangulation."

I shrugged. "That's how it felt."

My brother, Stuart, and I were having one of our regular Chinese restaurant sessions. The subtext was, as usual, that I should be more like him. He leads a more conventional life. He teaches at a state secondary school, and claims to find it more rewarding than he imagines academia would be. And who am I to say he's lying? I can only speak for myself but I'm glad I don't teach children. Stuart seems to spend about thirty per cent of his time waiting for kids to shut up. He likes to amuse me by showing me his classroom persona, in which he narrows his eyes like Clint Eastwood and says through clenched teeth, "I don't shout over children." I bet he does though. I bet he has to.

Stuart claims to enjoy teaching kids who aren't very bright, and I'm not sure I believe him. I think it's an assumption he has about himself that he doesn't dare to challenge, like that he's left-wing. Because the implications are disturbing, aren't they? You want to like the thick kids just as much, because life is less tragic and unfair if you do. Stuart, I suspect, holds some uncomfortable truths at arm's length. He's married, and to be happily married, unless you're extremely lucky or talented at marriage, I think you have to hold certain uncomfortable truths at arm's length. You want your beliefs and your emotions to corroborate where you've ended up, and that's bound to involve some well-meant self-deception. It won't surprise you to learn that, if Stuart is going to enjoy a novel, he has to *like the characters.*

He folded his arms across his paunch and looked at me. "How *is* Penny?"

"Fine." He was trying to make me feel guilty and he was almost succeeding.

"Enjoying the privilege of a monogamous Al?"

"Not really."

Stuart sighed. "So, are you still limiting yourself to the mature ones?"

"Yes, actually. More mature than me, if you must

144

know."

"Good. A man of principle."

"That's me."

"And how will you know when you've found the right one?"

"Who says I'm looking?"

It's not that Stuart is unimaginative – he writes pretty good nature poetry, which he self-publishes. But he is one of these people who are always trying to hurry you on the next stage – job, promotion, marriage, house, children, bigger house …

"So, you're just enjoying yourself?"

"It's what life's for."

"And is this fair on Penny?"

I winced. *"How smart a lash,"* I said, *"That speech doth give my conscience."* I refilled my wine glass, held the bottle over his. He shook his head: Driving. "All the more for me. Okay, so you mean I should either dump her or be faithful to her? Neither of which I seem capable of."

"Oh, I think you're capable, Al. You'll manage one of the two. One way or another. Hey, maybe the

145

house is just what you need. Maybe you'll feel more committed then."

"Maybe."

Neither of us sounded convinced. Then the food arrived – pork for me; chicken for Stuart, who was trying to lose weight again.

We ate in silence for a bit.

"How's the chicken?"

"Mm. Tender. Plenty of ginger. Bit oily."

"Well, that's what it's all about. According to you."

He frowned.

"*It's all about oil.*" I winked at him.

"Well, it *is*."

"Is it bollocks."

And I managed to forget about Penny for the rest of the meal, drinking the rest of the wine, needling Stuart with opinions I only half-held, bickering contentedly about the impending deaths of thousands.

4.

Josephine made an appointment with me via email. She didn't leave a clue as to what it was about, and I didn't press it. They read your emails, and I'm cautious enough not to expose anything in them. Was this about her assignment on misogyny in *Macbeth*? or the unfortunate incident of the leaky condom? I was in my office, trying to mark a terrible short story by a first year - all directionless dream sequences and transparent sexual fantasising - when there was a knock on my door. Josephine, early? No, that was a male knock. I put down the story with some relief and opened the door to Prentice.

"Have you got a minute?"

"Well, I'm expecting someone. Can it wait?"

"I just want to try out this idea about guilt."

"Guilt in *Macbeth*?"

He hesitated. "Sure."

I gave him a look as if to convey that this had better not be about that nonsense from the other day, and let him in.

"I've just spent the night with the Welsh girl," he said as soon as he'd sat down.

I folded my arms, leaned back. A Stuartesque gesture.

"I looked her up on Facebook, got chatting, she asked me to a party at her halls, and that was it. I slept with her last night. Sort of."

"You don't fancy the Welsh girl," I said. "Who I presume has a name."

"Holly. I told you. I know, but … You disapprove, don't you?"

"I'm uncomfortable about this whole thing. I'm worried about your reasons for doing it. And I still don't understand what *I've* got to do with all of -"

His phone had cheaped; he retrieved it from his pocket.

"Oh shit, it's her." He looked conflicted, and his large-eyed gaze came to rest on me as if I could give him an answer. Me, of all people.

"Prentice, did you sleep with her because you wanted to find out more about this – this 'murder' thing?"

148

"Sort of, yeah."

"And now she thinks you're her boyfriend?"

He blushed and looked down.

"What the hell are you doing?"

"She wants to meet me in the Starbucks near the library. I'm tempted to go, you know. I mean, I didn't exactly interrogate her about it last night or this morning. I knew that would look a bit weird. But I could ask her about it today, in Starbucks, and she'd probably tell me everything she knows."

You see a child picking a scab, your instinct is to stop them. I leant forward, elbows on my knees.

"Wait. Just think: What are you trying to achieve here? If you find out more about this guy, then what? What are you going to do about it?"

"Go to the police?"

"With no evidence."

"I could get some evidence."

"No, you couldn't. Prentice, listen. This is what you have to do. You have to text her back, tell her you're busy, and if she texts you again, tell her you've met someone else and you think you'd best not see her again.

149

Then you delete her on Facebook."

"Defriend?"

"Delete, defriend, whatever. Then you write your fucking essays."

"You're right. You're right."

"So do that, will you?"

There was a knock on my door, a polite knock which, I realised, had been preceded by female footsteps. I remembered Josephine's calves, her silver shoes, her sharp nails. I jumped up from my seat and opened the door. She was standing close, smiling in a relaxed way. Thank fuck, I thought, cautiously.

"Sorry, you're with someone."

"No, no. We said half-ten. Simon was just going."

She stepped aside to let him pass, which he did slowly, looking up at me. I caught a glance of complicity. As if just because I was shagging Josephine he could do whatever he wanted. I frowned back at him, saying, "Take my advice on that, Simon, and you won't go wrong."

Josephine stepped into my room and closed the door, leaning against it.

"Period," she said.

"Good."

She removed her glasses. "Kiss?"

I put my hands on her hips, slipped them up under her blouse. She gasped at the cold of my touch.

That afternoon I learned more about Josephine. She'd messed up in school, married young and years later felt the need for a second chance at education. She was amicably separated from her husband, who supported her pursuit of higher education. Now here she was in a flat he funded. She returned to the family home at weekends and in the holidays, but in the meantime the husband let her be, and there was no need for secrecy about what she got up to.

"It's terrible, Al, how much other women envy me. When I have sex with you, it's because I want to, not because it's a marital duty. And when I see my husband we're nice to each other, because we've not been squabbling about the domestic crap. I really think I've found a solution to the problem."

"Which problem's that? Security versus freedom?"

"Yes. Your dependable husband verses your sexy English professor. His greying chest hair notwithstanding."

She was straddling me, naked, post-coitally dishevelled, the late afternoon sun catching in her hair and her eyes.

"But what if you fall in love?"

She looked down at me, eyes widened in mock-horror. "OMG. With you?"

"With anyone. You don't think you'd want to live with a man again?"

"I prefer this. If I fall in love I can love the man – whether it's you or someone else – without having to live with him. I've done it, Al, and maybe it doesn't suit me. I'm not shirking love. I just don't want to live in the cage any more. Women want to trap a man into a home because of the maternal instinct. But for me, that work is done. My daughter's off to uni herself in three years. I can do whatever I like."

"Sounds like you've got it all figured out."

"So have you." She smirked, reached for the glass of Cava on the bedside table. The glass clashed against her grinning teeth. "You've got *Penny*."

5.

"Guess what?" Penny looked excited. I'd just sat down opposite her in the Starbucks above Borders Books. This was a house thing. What else would cause her eyes to shine like that?

"You've found somewhere you like."

"It's beautiful, Alex. It's perfect for us. Well, not perfect, I mean the downstairs loo needs a bit ..."

I watched her, rather than listened, remembering that I loved her enthusiasm and the way it animated her. In the early days it would have been a new play she'd seen. Now it was loft conversions, utility rooms, walls that could be 'knocked through' to form open-plan kitchen/dining rooms. This was growing up, I told myself.

"You don't sound too pleased," she said. A flash of anxiety in those auburn eyes. She had an autumnal look, Penny. A few years ago she had her colour profile done by someone who'd clearly known their stuff. The dark greens and greys of her blouses and scarves suited her fox-coloured hair. It was her eyes that I particularly relished, though. They were iridescent with shades of yellow, green and brown. It was with a jolt of desire, as well as a tactical avoidance of her question, that I leaned forward and kissed her.

"I'm delighted. I'm just gagging for a coffee. Do you want anything?"

In the queue I tried to feel pleased about what was happening. All her arguments made sense. She was right that renting was a waste of money when that same money could be invested in a property whose value was sure to rise for as far into the future as anyone could see. She was right that we were getting on. Did I want to be a father of a ten-year-old when I was fifty? And it was true that I loved her. But it was also true that I'd spent the afternoon having sex with a mature student when I should have been marking first-year short stories. My brother was right, I was a commitment-phobe. But then wasn't a phobia an *ir*rational fear? And weren't there rational grounds for fearing a financial entanglement with someone who might one day decide she hates you, who might well actually hate you *now* if she knew, for example, how you'd spent the afternoon? I caught sight of myself in the mirror behind the counter. My greying hair was too long. I was too old for this leather jacket. Even the slim, muscular body was beginning to look less like the result of good health and fortune, and more like a middle-aged man's vanity.

Penny explained more about the house, which we were going to see, or 'view', as Penny put it, as soon as I'd finished my coffee. Once, I thought, I would have found her assimilation of estate agents' jargon endearing. She leaned forward and put her face in her hands, elbows resting on the table. I remembered her looking at me like this on our first date, nearly four years previously, in the bar across the road from the theatre where she still worked. Now I felt uneasy under the scrutiny of her gaze, as if those glittering eyes might find me out.

"So, anyway," she said. "How was your day?"

I made her laugh by quoting some of the sexy bits from the first years' stories.

"But there's something very strange going on with one of my second years. This boy, Simon Prentice, he's started to -"

I'd lost her. She was smiling at something over my shoulder. I glanced round and saw a young man lifting a baby from a buggy to a high chair.

"So cute. Sorry. Go on, I'm listening."

"Forget it," I said. My coffee was finished. I regretted the extra shot, which had made me feel brittle and nervy. "Come on, then. Let's view this property."

6.

The next morning, I had just dismissed my first seminar group and was bracing myself for another session with the first year short stories, when the shaggy, bespectacled head of a colleague peered round my door.

"Morning, Jake. To what do I owe the pleasure?"

Jake was on an exchange programme and was due to return to Connecticut at the end of the year. I'd miss him. He was leaning against my desk, picking a white cat hair off his brown knitted tie. Was this something to do with Josephine?

"There is something rotten," he said, "in the state of bearded corpulence."

"Do you refer to our venerable head of department?" I said, getting into the spirit of the game, but still nervous.

"The very same. The Bloat King has spoken. Seen you his email?"

"Nay. What fresh hell *is* this? What's that file

you're holding?"

"These are essays by students who are going to be moved into your *Macbeth* group. They're chemistry students."

"What the fuck?"

"Welcome to the new system. Diversity. It seems the Bloat King is getting cross-curricular on your ass."

"This is ridiculous."

"He's given students from outside the subject area the opportunity to experience the joys of literature. They had to apply by submitting an essay, but still. You should see the bunch of jokers *I've* got for screen writing. I mean, you can imagine, right? One minute I'm thinking I'm going to get 60 per cent firsts out of this class. The next? I'm up to my ass in *sports scientists*."

"They'll fail."

"They're not allowed to. We're gonna have to dumb down, dude. I had a glance through yours." That was another thing. He'd read anything. He'd never say he didn't have the time. Short story students submitted novels to him and he read them all. He had no girlfriend, though. Not one. "Some of them are like GCSE papers.

159

A couple are perspective-merchants. There's one guy who argues that *Macbeth* is really the story of his triumph over bourgeois morality."

I groaned.

"It's not as bad as it sounds. Here we are. Liam Corbett. Read from there."

I read.

"Macbeth is essentially the story of one man's transcendence of Christian morality. The hero's trajectory can be read – indeed *should* be read – as a journey from human 'sin' and 'guilt' to a superhuman state of grace. The 'walking shadow' soliloquy, in which – according to critical orthodoxy - Macbeth laments the shallowness of life, is in fact a lucid account of life's insignificance, and therefore of the rightness of his murderous actions. Indeed, 'murder' is too pejorative a term for what Macbeth achieves ...”

I chucked it on my desk. "Don't get me started. Since when did deliberately misreading a text become officially an intelligent thing to do?"

"Since, I don't know, like 1970? At least the guy's *thought* about it."

"But he's so obviously *wrong*."

Jake smirked. "That's just your opinion, arrived at via your bourgeois assumptions of morality and your veneration of the dead, white, male canon and shit."

"So Shakespeare was really thinking that Macbeth was morally justified in ..."

"Hey, hey. Who cares what *Shakespeare* was thinking? I mean, he's just the *author*, right? And whose morality anyway?"

We were both chuckling by now.

"You enjoy talking crap, don't you?"

"Working here? For the Bloat King? I think you have to. It's the future." He let out an exasperated sigh, chucking the file onto my desk. "Al, if you want to have a job next year, you must try to pass as many of these assholes as you can. The email instructs us to 'mark positively'."

"It's political correctness gone mad."

"You said it, buddy."

So I set aside the first year short stories and attacked the file, beginning with Liam Corbett's justification of Macbeth's murders. I read it slowly, stopping to get up and pace about in my small, cramped office, cursing. Then I sat down at the computer, called up the students database and typed in Liam Corbett's name. A handsome, smirking blonde head bobbed into view. I checked my timetable. First thing tomorrow, he'd be in my seminar, with Prentice.

7

"Life's but a walking shadow," read Sarah, my best reader, *"a poor player / that struts and frets his hour upon the stage / And then is heard no more; it is a Tale / Told by an idiot, full of sound and fury / Signifying nothing."*

This speech rarely failed to make my eyes water, and I blinked rapidly as I asked the class, "Okay, so what's Macbeth saying?"

I glanced around the table. A bit thin on the ground today. The Beats Against Bush event had been followed by another, less official piss-up. The Australian girl, Ricki, was frowning, chewing gum and taking sips of an energy drink that I shouldn't have let her get away with but couldn't be bothered to challenge her over. Josephine was wearing her glasses, sensible shoes and a rather stiff cardigan, but there was nothing stiff about the gleam in her eye when I glanced at her. Prentice looked gaunt, hair sticking up as if he'd had a night of fretful sleep. Or fretful sex with what's-her-

163

name.

"What do you think, Ricki?" I said.

"It's like he's not bothered? He's like, my wife's dead, whatever."

"Okay, and where's your evidence for that?"

I wasn't expecting much, and was about to go to someone else, when Ricki said, "Like the whole rhythm of it. It's like blah blah blah bum ... Y'know? It's ... flat. Like depressed?"

"Yes."

"Cause he's like supped so full of horrors, like he was just saying when he heard the cry of women? And now it's like, nothing can touch him. But not, y'know, in a good way?"

"Yes."

Prentice was nodding. He made a note. He was distracted by a cough from Liam, who sat with his legs splayed, his gym-fit body swathed in a tight white T-shirt. Liam seemed to feel him looking and glanced up sharply. Prentice looked down at his notes.

"Liam?"

Liam looked up at me, chewing the end of his

pen. I heard Sabrina, the looker, giggle. Still watching Liam chewing his pen, I sensed her re-crossing her legs, tossing her hair, appealing to the new alpha male in the room. Liam was still staring at me, the insolent prick. My brother Graham must get this shit all the time.

"Maybe we'll come back to Liam. Er … Simon."

"I just *love* this series of metaphors," said Prentice. "The walking shadow. The poor player who struts his hour upon the stage and then gets forgotten. And then the weird bit at the end. Full of sound and fury. Signifying nothing." He shook his head, visibly moved, then glanced around as self-consciousness returned. Sabrina was smirking, Liam pretending to suppress hilarity, palm over his mouth.

"It's fantastic isn't it? It's amazing how much better it can make you feel when you find your own sense of futility expressed by an amazing writer. Beats a double scotch," I nodded at the hung-over Ricki "– *almost*."

"I'm more of a tequila gal."

A ripple of knowing laughter. Good, I'd rescued Prentice. For now.

"Okay so let's go back to this idea that he's incapable of feeling now."

"I just think he's a bastard," Sabrina said crossly. "I mean his wife's died and he's like, not thinking about her, just how he's lost his feelings. But I feel more sorry for *her*."

"Well isn't the depression caused by her death?" I said, but Prentice had cut in over me, louder.

"But isn't that what depression's like?" he said. "You become so focused on your own misery that you can't relate to others?"

Sabrina frowned as if Prentice had said something stupid – her usual reaction to a comment that went above her head.

I said, "There's a Freudian idea that you can't repress one emotion without repressing them all. Sound familiar? I included Liam with my glance. His answering stare gave nothing away.

"Maybe that's why their love for each other seems to die. They repress their guilt, and then they can't love."

"Have you any experience with that?" Liam was pointing at me with his pen.

I let the silence build for a moment. Then I said, "Sure. Happens to me all the time. How about you?"

"How about me what?"

"What do you think of this passage?"

"I think it's bullshit."

There was shocked laughter from the girls. I caught Josephine's eye and felt better when, keeping very still, she winked at me.

"Go on."

"Bullshit."

"So you said. Can you expand on that? In the sort of vocabulary that would be appropriate for an essay? I've read your stuff, Liam. I know you can do better."

"You've read my stuff?"

"Yeah."

A mischievous smile. Oh God. He thought he was shocking, subversive.

"Right." He had a northern accent. Leeds or possibly Sheffield. "If you're soooo depressed that you can't even grieve for your wife when she's just killed herself, you wouldn't be able to come out with - " He glanced at Prentice "- a series of really brilliant metaphors. So when I read this, I know it's not Macbeth saying all that walking shadow shit, it's Shakespeare. I mean talk about *bull*shit." He picked up his copy of the play and turned it over in his pale, heavy hands. "It just doesn't work for me." He let the book fall. So Shakespeare had flunked the Liam test.

"You volunteered for the Shakespeare module," I reminded him. "You competed for it. And the essay that got you in here was – was very fluent."

Liam shrugged.

"I think you and I need to have a chat after this session."

"Can't. Got rugby training."

"Well in that case – Yes?"

My door had opened. One of the receptionists was looking at me anxiously, holding an imaginary phone to her ear.

I picked up the phone in my office.

"Your wife on line three," said the receptionist.

My *what?* I pressed a button.

"Hello?"

Penny chuckled. "Hi there, prof."

"Hello, Mrs."

"Just my little joke. I wanted to see how it felt."

"And how did it feel? Is everything okay, by the way?"

"Very good."

She really shouldn't have called me at work like this in a non-emergency, but that would have to wait. She was too happy to be angry with.

"Guess what? You remember that place I showed you online last night? On Dudgeon Street?"

I remembered looking at various photographs of interiors on her computer.

"Oh, yes?"

"I've got a viewing at four. Can you make it?"

"Should be able to."

"See you at the cafe opposite at ten-to? Oh, I'm so excited!"

As I hurried back to my seminar room I could hear from down the corridor that something was going on. When I walked in I caught Liam laughing.

Prentice was shouting, veins bulging in his neck. "Well maybe you should *let* it affect you. You might be a better *per*son!"

Sabrina had moved to sit next to Liam and now she put a hand over her mouth and trembled with silent mirth. Josephine was trying to take it all lightly, but you could hear the anxiety in her voice as she tried for a mumsy, "Calm down, boys."

I stood with my arms folded, doing my version of Stuart's Clint Eastwood face, until silence fell. Ten minutes left. Awkward. Too late to start something new, too early to begin wrapping up. I looked at Prentice's angry, wounded face and was strongly tempted to kick out Liam for the last part of the session. But I had so little to go on, officially, to justify so potentially inflammatory a move. And what would I do if he refused to budge? Call security?

"Okay. Five minutes' silent writing on your interpretation of this soliloquy. Then we'll feed back. Any questions, save them to the end."

I had another group straight afterwards. I set them going on group discussions and presentations, so I didn't have to do much, just circulate, prompting them while trying to pretend to myself that I didn't feel angry with Liam. I thought about Josephine, her winking eye behind the lens of her reading glasses, the hint of what lay in store for me when I could see her again.

Prentice was waiting for me in the corridor.

"So how do you like Liam?" His eyes shone with something like triumph.

"I think he'd benefit from taking a more open-minded approach to great literature."

Prentice leaned close to me. I could smell his hair gel, a clean, young, innocent smell. "It's him," he said.

"What, you mean -?"

Prentice glanced over his shoulder and then did something I later wished he hadn't. He raised his palms in front of his chest and, wearing a mask of amused contempt, a spookily accurate mimicry of Liam's sneer, pushed his hands forward. He looked at my face, and something in it made him laugh strangely.

8.

"What you do then is put in a cheeky offer. I mean, it would need some work. But we could do a lot ourselves. We'd just need to resign ourselves to spending a lot of our weekends and most of your summer break painting and – what do you call it? – grouting. You look doubtful."

We were back in the café opposite. I was drinking a ginger beer because it was the closest they had to the real thing; Penny was nibbling a brownie and sipping tea. Viewing the house and talking about buying it had put the sparkle in her iridescent eyes, but there was a flicker of anxiety as she looked at me now.

"Penny, I've never done anything like this before. I don't even know what grouting *is*. And this summer was the time I was supposed to be getting more published. It's been a while and I can tell the Bloat King thinks I'm not –"

"You learn, Alex. As with anything else. You learn as you go along. We'll do it together."

"Sure." I swilled the ice around in the remains of

172

my ginger beer. Penny's hand closed around mine, trapping my fingers against the glass.

"I know what your brother would say."

I looked up. She winked at me.

"He'd say you're being a commitment-phobe."

She ran her free hand through my hair, looked at it, ruffled it a bit more as if restyling it.

"Bit more grey at the sides there," she said. "Very distinguished."

I took her hand away from my hair, held it. "Way out of my comfort zone with this domestic stuff," I said.

"You'll be great. I'll give you the space you need. That utility room would easily convert into a study for you. And anyway."

She dropped her hand to the table, fiddled with a cracked finger nail. The espresso machine began to hiss. Penny's voice rose over the din. "It's not like we're getting any younger. And we're hardly going to get a better deal, are we?"

9.

I didn't have any great passion for the impending invasion of Iraq. I was far from sure that it wasn't a terrible idea that would backfire spectacularly, resulting in thousands of unnecessary deaths and making the world a more dangerous place. So how come I ended up having a row with Penny about it?

I was cooking a chilli and had just realised that the burning smell was the paper I'd accidentally dropped into the pan along with the minced beef. I was trying to get it out, stupidly, with my bare fingers and had scorched my thumb when Penny, sitting at my table with a glass of Shiraz said, "I've booked the morning off next Thursday. For the march."

Running my hand under the cold tap, I said, "And why have you done that?"

She shrugged. "Just. You know. Have you had raw meat on that chopping board?"

"What? No, that's – Oh, shit, yeah."

I fucked about with chopping boards and the celery and carrots and the soap and the hot water that always took too long to come on while Penny said, "I want to make my protest about the war, obviously. You could join me? Aren't some of the others going? Isn't Jake?"

"Jake has a very light timetable on Thursdays. He's going along more out of curiosity than an ambition to influence the course of history."

"You don't approve," she said.

"Marching won't change anything. Blair committed to this ages ago. Sorry, Mr President, all these marching students have changed my mind. I don't think so."

"But that doesn't mean we should just sit back and let it happen. Unless you want it to happen?"

The chopping board slipped through the tea towel onto the floor. The floor was dirty, so I rinsed the chopping board again, splashing some water onto my shirt.

"It's not that. I'm just not too keen on some of the people I'd be marching with. Have you actually checked out the Stop the War coalition? They're not pacifists, you know. They're just on the other side."

"And who's side is that?"

My hand throbbed. I reached for my own Shiraz

and glugged it. "Whoever's against the West."

"The West is about to do something terrible. Out of sheer greed."

"Ah." I took another slug of wine. "Oil?"

"Well, yeah." I had my back to her, but could imagine the shrug that went with this.

"You know, Iraq's oil is protected in a trust fund. It'll be used for rebuilding the economy after –"

"Yeah right. You believe that."

"And what do you believe, Penny? Is the oil going to be illegally exported to the UK? How exactly does this happen? Describe the process."

"I don't know. But it's well documented that it's about oil. Everybody knows."

I turned round. "Everybody knows. For fucks' sake, Penny, I wish you'd actually read the odd book or newspaper now and then instead of believing what 'everybody' knows."

She coloured. Her shoulders slumped. I became conscious of having way too much power over her, and that should have stopped me. "Sorry, Pen. I'm just so annoyed with the complacency of this generation. Beats

Against Bush. Jesus. I mean, they go to some shit like that and think it makes them nice people. They're morally in pieces." I attacked the mince with a wooden spoon. Stubborn pink strings of meat stuck together and I jabbed at them, turning them grey, doubly dead.

I heard Penny say, "So you have the monopoly on morality now."

It struck me as the sort of thing Liam Corbett might say. I turned to her and pointed at her with my wooden spoon, which dripped globs of tomato purée onto the floor. "And it's exactly *that* sort of thinking that's taught them there's no right and wrong. Universities have a lot to answer for."

"You think?"

"Yes. Look, we have a generation of people in power – in government, in schools, in journalism, the – the *intelligentsia*, who've been raised on this idea that nothing is better than anything else. Nothing means anything other than what we decide it means. Morality is an illusion. So you forget that there's such a thing as evil."

"Sounds a bit. I don't know. Born-Again

Christian. Do you want to turn that down a bit? It's burning."

"You know how Saddam deals with his enemies? He makes them watch their wives and daughters being gang raped. He feeds them to the shredder. This is what we're so pleased with ourselves for appeasing. Big slaps on the backs all round for tolerating *that* guy."

"You think Dubya is any better?"

"Yes. He's just a dangerous fool. He's not *evil*. Beats Against Bush. Marching. I mean, who *gives* a shit?"

"How else am I going to have my say?"

"You and Hamas. You and Hezbollah. You and George Galloway and Harold Fucking Pinter - Oh bollocks."

"What?"

"I forgot the kidney beans."

She sighed. "Alright, don't join me on the march then. I can tell you think this war is a wonderful idea. You're getting to be a real reactionary -"

"So it's *reactionary* to want to change the world? Interventionism is *reactionary*?"

"Maybe it's your age."

"Oh right. The age card. I was waiting for that. You can't beat me with the arguments so you tell me I'm wrong because I'm older than you."

"Only by, what, eight years? It doesn't bother me."

"Then why bring it up?"

"I didn't mean – Look, it's fine. You've read more about it than me so you must be right. No, thanks, no more wine for me. Where are you going? Stop. Al, just wait a second. We used to be able to discuss things. I mean, it used to be an interesting discussion without being a row. What's –? Oh, come on. *Please!*"

"I'm going for the fucking kidney beans."

She looked at me and there was an edge of contempt in her eyes. "Yeah, right."

I decided to take that as *permission* to go and cool off in the bar down the road. Half way there, striding through a nasty cold wind, I realised I'd forgotten my phone. Well, good. I imagined her calling me, hearing it ring on the kitchen table, wondering where I was, deciding it had been a mistake to insult me – No, even

179

before I reached the pub I knew I didn't seriously think she'd been insulting. This was about something else. And I wasn't going to solve it brooding alone in the pub. I jogged towards a bus pulling up at a stop, made the short ride to Josephine's street.

The wind had eased while I'd been on the bus, and I was able to picture a good night ahead: an hour or two with Josephine, then returning home contrite. Maybe tomorrow it would all look different, and I could kick the house thing into the long grass for a bit while I … worked out what I wanted to do.

There was a BMW parked outside her house. Maybe the husband was visiting with their daughter. Did I really want to walk in on that scene? I could always pretend I was just passing and needed to collect a text book I'd lent her. And if her husband guessed at the truth? Well, so what if he did? Josephine had made it clear that she was a free woman. A liberated woman of the much-derided West … My row with Penny simmered in my mind as I waited for the doorbell to be answered. I heard a male voice. Right, okay. So deal with it. The door opened. Josephine stood in a dressing gown without her glasses. Her hair was fluffed up and her lipstick smudged. It was the smell that did it, though. A familiar, salty smell mixed with something male.

"Oh shit," she said. "Sorry, Al. Bad time."

A figure approached down the hallway. Josephine began to close the door. I put an arm against it, heard a voice say, "It's alright, Jo, you've nothing to hide. Hello, prof. I don't believe you have an appointment."

Liam stood, bare-chested in jeans. He hooked his thumbs into his belt, below the cobbled belly, grinned at me.

"Just came to … I'll leave you to it."

Liam laughed, slapped his muscular thigh through the tight denim.

"Shush!" said Josephine, genuinely annoyed at Liam, it seemed. She turned to me. "Sorry, but – you know."

"You're a free woman."

"Indeed."

"That's right, Al," said Liam, appearing behind her, making her jump by doint something to her arse. "You leave us to it. We'll see you anon." And he raised

181

a palm at me, clasped and unclasped it, a child's parody of a farewell wave.

10.

The thing is, it wasn't the first time. Okay, so I might not have been in love with Josephine. But you can't tell me I wasn't in love once, with someone else. She was called Amanda McCarthy. She was eight years older than me and she broke my heart, causing me to self-medicate with drink, and if it hadn't been for certain people stepping in to save me and bend a few rules, I'd have failed my masters. Maybe being with someone I loved less violently seemed like a safe bet. And maybe that's why I was especially angry with Liam. He ripped open those old wounds, tore out the half-healed flesh and chucked it over his well-muscled shoulder with a big fucking smile on his smugly handsome face

I walked back into town, beginning to tremble. I ducked into a quiet bar and took a double Jamesons to a dimly lit booth where someone had left a copy of the Guardian. I tried to read the comment pages, summoning counter-arguments as if I really was the hawk that Penny seemed to have turned me into. But I couldn't concentrate. After a couple more of the Jamesons I had begun to formulate what seemed like an excellent idea.

I walked to the faculty of Media, Critical and Creative Arts, punched in the code on the third attempt and went up to my office, lights snapping on in the corridors, my lumbering reflection in the windows, the throb of Rock DJ from the union bar. Waiting for the computer to boot up, I paced my cramped office, real tiger-in-a-cage shit, chewing my nails, only just refraining from pounding my fist against the shelves. I found Liam's essay in the file and began typing bits into Google. It took longer than it should have done – my typing was a bit off – but eventually the phrase *'indeed murder is too pejorative a term for what Macbeth achieves'* brought up an essay by some Yank.

Before I could think better of it I banged out an email to Liam, calling it 'URGENT', locked up and went home, where Penny, having apparently dined on beanless chilli and then cleaned up the kitchen, was sleeping soundly in my bed.

11.

Then it was nine in the morning. I stared at my computer screen, at last night's email and at Liam's prompt reply - "OK" - and tried to remember what the hell I'd been thinking last night.

There was a sprightly knock on the door.

"Come in?" I reached for the remains of my coffee, in which I'd dissolved a frothing Solpedine.

Liam came in, grinning. His tight top showed off his muscular arms. I pictured them wrapped around Josephine, her plump calves closing over his thrusting back ...

As if he could read my mind, Liam laughed.

"Take a seat," I said, not looking at him, going for enigmatic. His essay was still out from last night and I took it now and leafed through it. The chair creaked as Liam sat down. If I kept leafing through his essay, maybe I'd think of something smart to say.

"Big night last night?"

I looked up. "Hmm?"

He sniffed the air.

I looked down at the essay. "This essay. It bears a remarkable resemblance to one I found online."

"You mean is it plagiarised? Bits of it, yeah."

"You do realise that's an offence under the code - "

"No no no, it's not. This isn't an assessed piece of work."

"It was what got you onto the Shakespeare module -"

"But it wasn't *ass-essed*. Not formally."

"But -"

"Prof. Before you go any further and embarrass yourself, a mate of mine was done for plagiarism last year and he got off because the essay he nabbed of tinternet wasn't *formally assessed*. It didn't count towards his final grade. This was an *exercise*."

"So you can steal whatever you like? Just cut and paste and that's fine as long as it's not technically towards your final credits?"

"Hey, I don't make the rules. I don't break them either. Well, if I did, I wouldn't get caught. So. If there's nothing else. I'm supposed to be meeting Jo for breakfast. Talking of breaking the rules. So. No hard feelings?"

I tossed the essay onto my desk, hoping to convey my contempt, but this was undermined by the shakiness of my voiced as I said, "We still have things to discuss, Liam."

"Like?"

"Well, your general – your general attitude, for one thing."

He leaned forward, as if to scrutinise my face for clues. He would have seen a hungover jilted lover, haemorrhaging authority.

"Why did you really call me in this morning? Do you even remember? Were you going to try to tell me that nothing was going on between you two? Or to try to persuade me to keep my mouth shut about it? Or to – I don't know – threaten me with a plagiarism charge so that I'd stop shagging her? I mean, my guess is that you don't quite know yourself. You don't exactly seem like a man with a plan, frankly." He cackled to himself, slapped his solid thigh. "She's gonna love this."

"We could talk about the murder."

187

"... The murder in *Macbeth*?"

There had been a pause. Not a long one, but still. We stared at each other. Something happened in his eyes. It's not the sort of thing that plays well in a police interview or a court of law, and you might think this was imagination, but I know that I saw a widening of the eyes, a dilation, then contraction of the pupils, and his neck tensed with the effort not to turn his head away.

"*This* shit again." He shook his head. "The things that follow you around. Well, as you know, there's no evidence for any of that, so. Who told you about that, by the way?"

I drained the coffee. Tiny white specks of codeine and paracetamol stuck to the bottom of the mug.

"Oh dear, prof's gone all quiet."

I was getting up, shuffling papers on my desk. What had I done?

"Not Jo. I don't *think*. Maybe – thingy. That Welsh girl with the big arse. Holly. No, hang on. That weird kid she's been shagging. The one in our – Simon! Simon Prentice. Ah, I deduce from your face, Dr Sherlock, that I have guessed correctly. Thanks for that.

Very useful info. And now if there's nothing else. She'll be waiting."

He stopped, his hand on the door knob.

"There's something about the older woman, don't you think? Well, maybe you don't notice because she's your age, but … They know how to get what they need. Without wanting to get too gynaecological -"

"Is this the bit where I'm supposed to lose my temper?"

"Ah, prof. Now I think you have just enough self-control left not to do anything quite *that* stupid. Oh well. I'll give her one from you. Ciao."

I locked the door behind him and sat, shaking until I had to go to my first class.

Why do we do the things we do? Shakespeare gave Macbeth his vaulting ambition, Lear his vanity, Othello his green-eyed monster. But what motivates most of our decisions *really*? One reason I found the all-about-oil cliché of the Iraq war irritating was because it was so unimaginative in its reading of motive. It reduced Bush and Blair to the status of burglars and bag-snatchers, whereas anyone paying attention could see that there were more grandiose motivations at play. That dangerous desire, so common in the powerful, to use violence to make the world a better place.

But what about those of us without much power? What motivates most of us? Love, sure. But often it's the path of least resistance, the desire for a quiet life. Fear of penury, of isolation. And of course lust. But when I look back on my behaviour during those weeks in 2003, I wish I could attribute it to some definable driving force. But it's the lesser, pettier emotions that I suspect were at play: Resentment; a nagging, vague status anxiety; a resurgent bitterness from the way I was treated by Amanda McCarthy; vindictiveness against someone who I felt to be my spiritual opposite, but who I feared was far closer to me than I liked to think. And of course the older man's sexual jealousy. Then there's the generalised malice that comes of self-pity. Like the Second Murderer in Macbeth: *"I am one, my Liege, Whom the vile Blows and Buffets of the World Hath so incens'd that I am reckless what I do to spight the world ..."* Then something deeper, more frightening and harder to face – an impulse to self-destruction and, within that, a desire to drag others down with me, just to feel less lonely as I fell.

12.

It's a requirement of the Shakespeare module that I give the students the option of taking some credits in Creative Writing. And so I decided to take them up the Cathedral. I'd done this before and it had always worked well, getting the less inspired ones past their fear of the blank page. You get into pairs, share your ideas, then write your first drafts. Then, after an interval of a few days, you return to the cathedral with your partner and redraft your first idea.

It was a clear spring day. I'd learned from experience that it was better to head up the rear on these trips than to lead and risk losing some while your back was turned. Liam strode ahead, defiantly coatless, his chunky buttocks in his tight jeans, his muscular arm at one point looping around the shoulders of Sabrina, the looker. You can handle this, I told myself. You're the adult here. My interview with Liam had shocked me into sobriety and I hadn't drunk all week. Not drinking also seemed to help to put the whole Liam-Prentice-

Josephine thing into perspective. And I'd apologised about the Iraq row to Penny, who'd officially forgiven me but was actually meek and sullen. The house situation I was putting off thinking about until tomorrow's Chinese session with Stuart, which I planned to use for getting my head together on the subject. As for Josephine, she wasn't here today, which might have been a coward's way of avoiding the awkwardness of the love triangle. I was relieved about that, while uneasy at the implications – *You see, Al,* I could imagine Stuart saying, *this is why you're not allowed to fuck them.*

The lights changed and I waited at the pelican crossing.

"Sorry to hear about Josephine and Liam."

Prentice was beside me, brushing a lock of hair from his face. His eyes were shining with something more than a reaction to the wind, which was getting harsher and colder as it blew up the wide street leading down to the docks.

"Holly and I are – are no more. It's funny, you kind of … You can't fake it, with a woman. Do you know what I mean?"

"Not entirely. So you didn't glean any more -?"

"No. But come on, Al. I mean, you can tell, can't you? You know it's true."

The lights changed; we crossed. Ricki was waiting on the other side, wanting to know if I'd marked her latest story.

As we waited for the lift to the top of the Cathedral it was no longer possible to pretend that this was a mild spring day. Liam jogged on the spot as if warming up before a game. Most of the rest were girls and were not quite dressed for it. There was a lot of covering of arms and shivering. I don't know if you remember, but the early 2000s was the era of the naked midriff. Even the chubbier of the girls had their navels, some of them pierced, exposed to the elements. The sight of all this bare, goose-pimpled flesh gave me an erotic kick, which was followed, quick as an echo, by the punch of sexual jealousy.

Ricki began passing round a flask. I could tell from the grimaces that it contained something more potent than tea. I turned a blind eye.

We emerged from the lift into a serious wind. It blew clouds over the city, casting dark shadows that prowled the town centre, the gridded suburbs, the explosions of green parks and, further out, the docks and the river. I let them take a minute to appreciate the sights, pointing out familiar landmarks, now defamiliarised by our lofty view.

Then I put them in pairs. Mostly I could let them choose. But when three of the girls asked if they could be a trio, Prentice was left, alone at the sidelines, and Liam paired up with Sabrina, I put my foot down. Over their protests I got Sabrina with Ricki and Liam with Prentice. The police asked about this decision later, and I told them I had hoped that, by working together, they would become friends. Which was a truth of sorts. I wanted to nail Liam at that point, and Prentice seemed to be the best route to achieving that.

I declared it time to get writing, and led by example, making a show of gazing across the city and scrawling in my notebook. The students started to shut up and get to work, conversation dying out, giving way to the whistling wind, punctuated by the clicking of lighters as the smokers struggled to spark up. There was the occasional muffled expletive as the wind flipped the pages of notebooks. Otherwise it was the odd police siren, the hiss and groan of distant traffic, the perennial seagulls. I always love this bit, the shifting non-silence of communal creativity.

I stopped pretending to make notes and actually started to make some. Last year I'd done a sort of Ted Hughes parody about a pigeon's eye-view of the city. Today I felt the pull of something more personal. Not Josephine; not allowed. So I looked to my past. If I turned north I could see the grim, crime-ridden area I'd lived before I knew better, when I first came here as an undergraduate. Further east was the less intimidating suburb which had been my home for the second and third years. Then poverty had compelled me, after my split with Amanda, to move into a bedsit closer to the centre, a period that had coincided with the area's notoriety for gang violence. A gut-shot gangster had collapsed against my door one night when I was working on my thesis. I'd helped him in, called an ambulance, and administered first aid in my cack-handed way. He'd survived and posted a Christmas card. As I'd opened the envelope, an eighth of skunk weed had slipped to my balding carpet. The bloody thing hung around, wedged in my copy of *Bleak House* until the day I got the thesis handed in, and I pretty much scotched that night's party by foolishly trying to smoke some of the stuff.

"Fancy a snifter?"

Ricki proffered her hip flask. I realised I'd walked around the turret, and was out of sight of most of the class now.

"Bit early for me."

"You know what time it is in Brisbane? Ten-thirty PM. When you think of it that way ..."

Ricki cocked a pierced eyebrow. There was also a ring in her belly button, I noticed. I imagined the ring's texture against my tongue, its salty taste.

"Alright, go on then." Stuart didn't get to do this. I took the flask and drank. "Woah!"

Ricki raised her arms above her head, swayed her hips, singing the ascending brass riff: "Ba-ba-ba-ba-ba-ba-BAH! Tequila!"

197

I returned the flask. "Read me what you've got."

Ricki opened her notebook. "It's about the Iraq war march next week? Here we go. *No blood for oil. Not in my name. Down with this sort of thing. The sheep bleat their slogans as they shamble and ramble down the valley of virtue towards an ever-decreasing pinprick of light. In a desert hoard, the nuclear arsenal gleams with malevolence as the dictator's smirk quivers beneath his darkly overhanging moustache.* Okay so it's a bit shit, but you know? First draft. Maybe glitters instead of quivers? More metallic, like the nuclear bombs?"

"Yeah, but 'quivers' has the connotation of an arsenal of weapons, as in quiver-full of arrows. Which I'm sure was deliberate."

"Of course. Absolutely. Glad you noticed."

"It's a good start, Ricki. So I take it you won't be among the 'sheep' next week?"

"I can't decide. One minute I'm like, what the fuck are we doing? The next I'm like, let's fucking *do* it. You know? Because – Shit, what was that?"

There was a commotion going on around the

corner. We hurried over and saw the rest of the students clustered near the wall – the chest-high wall that protected us from the lethal drop below. There was a burble of voices, male commands and female pleading, led by Sabrina's wail of ascending hysteria.

"Don't do it don't do it! Nooo!"

I pushed through the crowd. Prentice sat on the wall, his feet dangling into space, hands palms-down behind his narrow hips as if about to launch himself into space. I glanced around and saw Liam standing some way off, crouched in a rugby-like pose, as if about to hurl himself at Prentice. Liam caught my eye. His gaze was steady, mocking, detached.

"Simon, don't be an idiot," I said, walking towards him. He turned his head and looked at me, eyes ablaze. I felt light-headed, numb. On the edge of my vision I saw a shifting white shape, Liam's rugby shirt, circling to my right, keeping a clear route to Prentice.

"Is he gonna push me?"

"Liam!" I said, without taking my eyes from Prentice.

"Ready to grab him, prof," said Liam. "If needs

199

be."

"Thanks, Liam, but we're okay. Aren't we, Simon?" I was close enough now to touch him. "I'm going to put my hand on you now, okay?"

"This feels good," he said.

"It won't on the way down." I put my hand on his shoulder, felt the quivering muscle beneath the corduroy jacket. "Come on now."

He shuffled round, put his arms on my shoulders and made the short jump to the ground. There were voices, Sabrina making an exhibition of her relief, Liam laughing. There was jeering in the laughter, the derision of an underwhelmed spectator. I patted Prentice on the back. "It's okay," I said, though I've no idea what I meant by that. Keeping a hand on Prentice's shoulder, I led him away from the edge. An elderly couple, probably tourists, were gaping at us. I gave them a reassuring smile.

"Fuck me, that was scary," said Ricki. "What are you on?"

"Just wanted some inspiration," said Prentice. He gave Liam an unreadable look. "It's quite a buzz."

"Not to be repeated, I hope," I said, wanting to get the hell out of the Cathedral and onto ground level. "Come on, let's go. We must all have something to write about now."

I hung back. Prentice waited with me at the lights.

"What the hell were you thinking?"

"I think you can guess, Al. Did you see him?"

"What? Liam? You were testing Liam?"

"He was just dying for me to jump. He was ready to help me along."

"He was ready to save you."

Prentice looked at me.

"Simon, listen …" But the lights changed and he hurried across the road.

13.

I found Josephine standing by my door, a stack of books hugged to her chest like a girl in an American high school movie.

"Can we get a coffee?" she said.

She wasn't wearing her glasses, and I noticed as she led the way to her new favourite cafe that she'd got some new jeans. Was there an extra sway in her gait? How wrong I'd been earlier to think that this was behind me, that I could look out at the city and think about my recent past with a sense of proportion.

We sat down – Josephine with a coffee, me with a powerful Shiraz – and she got down to business.

"I just want to say that I'm sorry about the other night. I feel really bad about it."

But nothing in her demeanour suggested bad feeling. She was all glossy hair, glowing skin, clear eyes and – as she removed her tight-fitting leather jacket – thrusting breasts.

"Well. I hope you feel better having done so."

She laid a hand on my arm. "Don't be an arse."

I thought I was safe going for the mature ones. And I thought she would be too old for the Liams of this world. But why shouldn't he appreciate the very things about her that I did? It was bad enough knowing that Liam and I shared a taste in women. But what did she see in him?

"I can see that he's handsome," I said. "And fit. But is that all it takes with you? I mean, is this sexual liberation of yours really that shallow?"

"He's young. We all like the idea of someone younger. Including you, I bet. How old's what's-her-name? Penny?"

I didn't rise to that. "Young, handsome, fit. That's all?"

"No, that's not all. I like the way his mind works. Don't look at me like that."

"You like the way he shits on Shakespeare? You think that makes him intelligent."

"He questions things. Even morality. It's like, *whose* morality? And I can relate to that."

"Bloody hell."

She leaned forward, her pretty face twisting. "Listen. I spent years being good. A good little wife, then a good little mother, saving money to buy status symbols and swallowing the whole middle-class package. And what good did that do me? My husband *still* had an affair with his bloody secretary."

"Did he?"

"It's not that I didn't have temptations."

"I'm sure you did."

"You bet I did. And I resisted them. Because it was the right thing to do."

"Sometimes there *is* a right thing to do."

She looked up at me, softer now. "I know. But … It can just turn out not to do you any good. Then I come here and I meet you and you help me to remember how wonderful literature is. And I meet *him* and it's like – tearing up everything. It's exciting. And he puts it into context. You know, he said, is it any wonder I want to forge my own path, morally, when the people in charge are so corrupt? You know, the prime minister is joining the stupidest president in history in an illegal, colonialist war which is all about oil, and yet the rest of us are supposed to behave? Once you see through that hypocrisy, it's liberating -"

"Oh, shit, Jo."

"What?"

"I didn't realise you were like *this*."

"Neither did I! But it seems I am. And I'm so

grateful to you, Al, for … shaking me loose. You liberated me. I'll never forget that."

I had to look away from her, and to pull my hand away from hers. Ricki was at a table in the corner, a bottle of beer on the go, scribbling in her notebook.

Josephine had followed my gaze and was now giving me a conspiratorial look.

"He was all over one of the girls in my class today. Sabrina. The looker."

Josephine looked stung, but controlled herself. "So what if he was? I don't have any claim over him just as he doesn't over me."

"Good. Fine. Just saying."

"Sure you are, Al." She began putting her purse into her handbag. That looked new, and expensive. But what did I know about handbags?

"How does he afford the BMW?"

That stopped her. She looked at me, head on one side.

"Ouch! Status anxiety? From my esteemed literature professor? Whose mind should be on higher things?"

"It's not that. There's … There's a rumour about him."

"A rumour. Wow." She was angry about Sabrina, I thought.

"I'm telling you this for your own protection. My motivation here is your safety. Okay?"

She looked doubtful. "So what's this rumour?"

"The rumour is -" Across the bar, I saw Ricki chewing her pen, scoring the label of her bottle of Peroni. She saw me looking, waved. I smiled, nodded. I almost got up and went over to her. But when I glanced back at Josephine, her face appeared so smug that, just to see her expression change, I continued. "The rumour is: A few years ago, Liam killed someone. He pushed an old woman down the stairs, to get his hands on her will. I mean he took a cut of her will."

"*What*? Who was -?"

"I don't know."

"Where did this -? How did -?"

"I don't know. All I know is what I've told you. But I have it on good authority."

"Really? Like, the police, or … ?"

"Another student."

She looked at me and began to smile, not nicely. "You really are quite pathetic, aren't you? You're an overgrown, lost little boy." She took a last sip of her coffee.   "Tell you what. I'll ask him, shall I?"

"No! Don't let him know you know. You'll put yourself in danger. You mustn't -"

"I'm sure the university has some sort of counselling service, Al. I've said what I came here to say. Now if you'll excuse me, I have a lecture to go to." She nodded at my empty wine glass. "Perhaps you do too."

14.

As I passed reception, the new girl said, "What happened on the Cathedral today?"

I realised I had to report it. I filled in the requisite form, and thought it was this that was to be discussed when I got an email summoning me to the office of the Douglas Blunt, our head of department, or The Bloat King as Jake had it.

He took me through the incident and said he'd refer Prentice to the pastoral team. "Someone will be in touch."

"I know him quite well. He's ..."

The Bloat King inclined his head. "Yes?"

Now was my chance. I could simply tell him everything. What stopped me was this: If I told him about Simon's fears about Liam, Liam and probably Josephine would accuse me of a malicious slander motivated by jealousy. Jealousy over what exactly? the Bloat King would ask, and would have no choice but to report our affair and then ... It was all too easy to imagine the university forgetting a vague and remote murder allegation when tempted by the giddy prospect of sacking a sexually misbehaving professor.

Impossible to say how much of this train of thought the Bloat King followed, or what he already knew or intuited. "Hmm. You know him well. Right. Now, about that sort of thing, Alex." He shifted about in his chair, causing it to creak, folded his arms across his narrow chest, resting them on the pillow of his white-shirted gut. "There's … There's a growing perception that you're a bit *too* close. Things are noticed."

"I always get nervous," I said, to cover my nerves, "When you lapse into the passive tense."

He smiled, then removed his glasses, examined them, and replaced them, peering at me soberly. "They're still basically children and they're in our care. And we need to –" He raised his palms, in a gesture that reminded me of Prentice's rendering of Liam's push. I looked at the dry white palms, the swollen flesh around the wedding ring.

"I know. I do. I do keep a distance."

The Bloat King puffed out a breath of air, a sort of

verbal fart of mild contempt. He sat back and folded his hands on his belly, breathing through his nose. Either deciding what to say or allowing me a chance to say more.

"Not all of them are children."

"No," he said, bowing his head in concession. "Some of the mature ones are – well, they're mature. And I appreciate that you seem to make that distinction. As far as I know. So far. But there is still such a thing as a code of conduct. And there is such a thing as summary dismissal for its breach. Do we understand each other?"

"Not sure. Are you saying -?"

"Alex, your results get better each year. The students enjoy your classes; you have high attendance. I appreciate the way you filled in for Jake when he was off last term. And I still hope to see you publish more work. And, you even put up with some of my more -" A self-deprecating chuckle "- controversial … experiments, shall we say. I give you sports scientists, you take them without complaint. I appreciate that. You're not someone I'd be happy to lose. Or, to put it another way, if I wanted to lose you, I would have done already. I have more than enough material. I mean, do I have to keep putting this in different ways and embarrassing us both or –?"

"No. No. I get it."

"Is there anything more you can say that might reassure me?"

"I am not in a sexual relationship with any of my students. How's that?"

He looked at me and I could see my honesty was noticed. Then he raised a finger at me. "Keep it that way."

He slapped my shoulder as he showed me out.

15.

I walked home. Tomorrow was the day of the Iraq war march and the university would be closed. I passed the police cordons, the signs for diverted traffic, and allowed the humiliation with Josephine to settle. It was a humbling, necessary corrective. And my session with the Bloat King had been a timely demonstration of the futility of all such relationships. I was thinking I'd get in, change into my tracksuit and go for a long, head-clearing run in the park. But I arrived to find Penny making coffee in the kitchen.

"Afternoon." she said. She was wearing my dressing gown. Her hair was matted from bed. "Free for the rest of the day?"

"Yep."

"Me too. Coffee?"

I came up behind her, slipped my arms around her. "I'm sorry."

She turned around and looked up at me.

"You've been terrible."

I put my arms around her and lifted her onto the counter.

"You've been shocking."

We kissed. She said, close to my ear. "What's going on with us?"

"A fresh start."

"I didn't take my pill? Last night. I thought -" Her autumnal eyes flooded with tears. "I thought it was over for us."

I kissed the tears from the corners of her eyes. "It's not over. Let's buy this house. Let's have a child."

She gasped and cried some more, then pushed herself off the counter and led me to the bedroom.

16.

At the start of the march, someone handed us a placard, a white board on which the words NOT IN MY NAME were scrawled. I enjoyed not commenting on the narcissism of the slogan, and gamely held it aloft, my free hand taking Penny's and feeling it squeeze. Maybe this is how it's done. You suppress your doubts and make yourself play the part – the monogamous homemaker, the righteous protester – until it becomes you. We began marching, though at a slow, petty pace, more strolling than marching. This was a day out, a chance to enjoy the city in fine weather among like-minded people. Through the crowd I saw Jake, standing at the side lines with a camera. He raised it, I gave him a shit-eating grin and he snapped a photograph. I allowed myself to be swept along with the pleasure of submission. This was conformity, and it was a relief. The protests were being held all over the country. The one planned for London next week was expected to break records. And who knew? Maybe Blair would take note after all. Regardless of his commitment to Bush, he might come round. Then Bush would lose heart and call off the troops. And Saddam, freed from the macho imperative to defy the West, would voluntarily surrender his weapons. Well, anyway. *I* would not be asked to fight. While Iraq burned, I would be making love to Penny, getting Penny pregnant, buying the house, embracing maturity. I could still publish something this summer. Maybe nothing to do with *Macbeth*. Why continue my immersion in all that evil?

My phone vibrated in my pocket. Telling myself I wasn't hoping it would be Josephine, I said to Penny, "Fancy a turn with this?"

She smiled and took the placard. I quickly checked my phone. The number was one I didn't recognise. The text said: "We're heading to the Cathedral now. It's him or me – Simon."

How had he got my number? From Liam? Who got it from Josephine? I called. Straight to voicemail. I started running, ignoring Penny's voice, rising over the chattering and chanting of the marchers. I pushed on through, elbowing my way past a group of T-shirted young men, an older couple, a young cop who for a minute looked like he fancied giving chase. I stumbled on a kerb, crashed into a young woman who dropped her placard. NO BLOOD FOR OIL shouted up at me from the pavement as she swore behind me. I pushed on, calling again, hearing the mechanical voice and leaving a message - "Simon. Call me now. I'm nearly there. Just don't go up. Call me." I saw Ricki, passing her hip flask, raising a fist and pumping the air, chanting a slogan that was lost in the general babble.

"Ricki!"

"Hello, prof. Nice to see another sceptic. I finished my poem. Fancy a snifter?"

"Have you seen Simon? Liam?"

She shook her head. "They're not coming. They were doing the thing."

"What thing?"

"They were meeting up today. They're a pair, yeah? Simon said he wasn't bothered about the march and neither was Liam. They were going to meet."

"At the Cathedral?"

She shrugged. "I guess."

I ran on, approaching the front now, where the marchers were more serious. There was an atmosphere of aggression, genuine anger in their scowling faces, their up-thrusting arms, their chanting voices. There were fewer women, more police.

"Everything okay, sir?"

A police officer had fallen in beside me.

"I want to go up the Cathedral."

"It's closed for the day."

I ran on.

The cathedral was blocked off, guarded by mounted police. I circled it, breaking away from the march, which snaked its way around the square. There were police guards, horses, closed doors. If I couldn't get in, neither could they. Thank fuck. Him or me? What an idiot. Right, that did it. I was definitely reporting this. I went back to join the march, now having to deal with a different problem – moving back, swimming against the tide of protesters - to find Penny. I don't know what it was that made me look back. Perhaps I saw a look on someone's face, a horrified or disbelieving stare ...

The sight was strangely familiar. For the last two

years, during the gestation of the coming war, we'd revisited time and again an image of its provocation. Now I was looking at something similar: A body, a slight, dark-haired man, windmilling down, next to a straight, concrete edge and, some five or ten body-lengths above it, a second body, a muscular, blonde man, this one taking a more direct head-first plunge. They accelerated as they went, their descent seeming to cause the rising note of horror in the voices around me. I was close enough to just feel the tremor as they landed, to see two gentle puffs of pink vapour.

17.

The coroner recorded an open verdict. So what happened? Try this: Prentice lures Liam up there with the intention of killing him. A struggle ensues. Liam, being stronger and, possibly, an experienced killer, gets the upper hand, but Prentice drags him down with him.

Don't buy the theory of Prentice as killer? Well here's another, more potent than the first: Liam, knowing that Prentice knows about the murder (because he read this in my stupid hungover face that morning) intends to kill Prentice. He attempts to throw Prentice off the Cathedral, but a struggle ensues. Both men topple to their deaths.

Then there's this, my personal favourite because its psychological weirdness rings truer than the neater theories: Prentice, in some confused corner of his soul, intends for Liam to kill him, because that would prove that Liam is a killer. His bizarre stunt at the top of the cathedral during our writing exercise was a rehearsal for this, or a spontaneous flirting with death that gave him the idea for getting Liam to kill him. However, once he is there, and Liam is pushing him over the edge, instinct kicks in. Clarity is restored. What the hell is he doing? He has to survive! So grapples with his assailant. Liam, terrified that the attempt but not the deed confounds him, pushes Prentice harder and in the process loses his balance - Both men fall …

His text to me? A mystery. A mystery and a torment. Like these questions I was asked.

Did you not have a suspicion that Mr Prentice's life was in danger?

Did you ever raise with the police the prospect that Mr Corbett could be a murderer?

Did you do everything within your power to discourage the association between the vulnerable Mr Prentice and the possibly murderous Mr Corbett?

Are you quite satisfied that you had no power to avert this tragedy?

Was it not your jealousy of Mr Corbett that motivated you when you encouraged the partnership between Mr Corbett and Mr Prentice?

And was it not your fear of the exposure of your affair with a student that prevented you from reporting the allegation?

I answered as honestly as I could, even managing to face Jenny as she issued horrified gasps from the public gallery. I hated the look of disillusionment on her pale, hardening face, as if she were ageing before my eyes. And why hadn't I told her before? Sheer cowardice, and a pathetic hope of getting away with *some*thing. Then Josephine took the stand and she was honest too. Oh, yes she was very candid indeed. She'd seen Liam off that morning. He'd been happy, relaxed and, presumably, well fucked. But her evidence did little to explain the deaths.

Penny drove me home in silence. Then she came in behind me and began banging around my flat, gathering her stuff.

"The worst thing," she said, as she chucked her books and CDs into a cardboard box, "is not the affair. It's what you did with that poor boy."

"But I hardly did anything -"

Even before the words were out of my mouth I knew what she'd say: "Exactly!"

221

18.

The police charged me with Criminal Negligence, but the CPS chose not to prosecute. There was a bit of a media shitstorm about that. Two young men dead and no-one held to account. But what could be done about it now?

I was suspended from the university pending the inquest, and afterwards, was summoned by a phone call to meet the vice chancellor. Here we go. Then the Bloat King's secretary rang me, scheduling a meeting half an hour before the other.

The secretary barely met my eye as she showed me in. The Bloat King shook my hand and sat down, smoothing his tie over his paunch, with the furrowed look that decent men tend to have when they're about to cause pain.

"You're appointment's at four, isn't it? I suppose you know what's coming."

"I can imagine."

"I'm afraid I support the decision to let you go,

Alex. The affair, the publicity, it's too much."

I almost felt sorry for him. He must have done this before, or things like it. But he was clearly finding it hard. And me? A numbness had descended. It was as if I was watching us from the far corner of the room. But then he twisted about in his chair and added, "And I've just had Mrs Prentice on the phone and … Look, I'll write you a good reference, in all sincerity about your – your skills. But I can't vouch for ..."

"My character."

"Well. I'm sorry, Alex. I mean I did warn you. It's not as if …"

"What did she say? Simon's mum?"

"Well, she was very angry that the university didn't do more to step in and prevent his death."

"Meaning me."

"Well not just you. Actually she said something else. Simon wrote to her. Old-fashioned letters he'd send in the post. He often mentioned you. Apparently he thought you were great. Said you understood him and cared about him, made him realise what was wonderful about Shakespeare. That sort of – Oh. Oh, hold on."

He delved in his desk drawers for a bit until he found a pack of pocket tissues, began to withdraw one, then changed his mind and tossed the pack gently across his clear, polished desk.

"I'm sorry," I said when I could speak again. I meant for puting him through the embarrassment but he seemed to take it in a more general way.

"I appreciate that. And I wish I could … I wish things were different. But- Excuse me."

He picked up the receiver of his phone, which had begun to ring. "Yes? … Take a message. And hold my calls for now. Thanks." He hung up. "Can I trust you with something?"

"Of course."

"The police have been around quite a bit, and they're not giving much away, but one of the receptionists overheard them. They hear a lot, the girls in there. People forget they have ears and minds of their own. Anyway. They think Liam did it. The murder. There was a verdict of accidental death. Old ladies fall down the stairs all the time of course. But it's his finances that are raising questions. I imagine it will take some time. Anyway, you'll know more when I do."

The numbness had gone. I was cold, quivering. After a moment the Bloat King rose from his chair. He waddled around the desk, patting my shoulder, and opened the bottom drawer of his filing cabinet.

"I won this in the Christmas raffle. I knew it would come in handy. I'm afraid we'll have to drink from these."

He poured two shots of Scotch into paper cups and brought them back to the desk. We sat and drank, mostly in silence as the room got dark.

"It's not our world, is it?" I said. "Murder. I spend my days steeped in *Macbeth* and then when there's a real one right under my nose, it doesn't seem real."

"I know."

He refilled my cup. We sipped our drinks while the minute hand crept up to 12 and my session with the vice chancellor. The Scotch went down so well that I bought myself a bottle on the way home.

19.

Things could be worse. I'm still in the flat. I'm burning through an ISA that I've had waiting for a rainy day since my rich uncle died five years ago. It was going to go on the deposit for the house with Penny, and there's enough of it to keep me in baked beans and whisky for another couple of months. Then I'll have to give up the flat and move to a cheaper one in the dodgy part of town that I lived in during my masters. I still apply for the odd job now and then, though I've yet to be called for an interview, surprise surprise. (I picture them noticing my name on the application, remembering where they've heard it, calling out across the office. *Hey, guys, guess who's applied ...*)

At first I spent a lot of time drinking in bed, reading or watching TV. You can get 24-hour coverage of the war. I check in now and then, to see how it's going. There's something strangely soothing about the muted thuds and infra-red flashes of Shock and Awe. The shock, I find, wears off pretty quickly, but the awe endures.

Stuart made a nuisance of himself, of course. I stopped answering his calls, so he came round - at rather a bad time. I'm afraid we parted on not very good terms. The trouble was, he seemed to think he'd been proved right about something. But the next day I noticed he'd put a fair bit of money in my account. I'll make it up to him. Promise.

Then I tried becoming a 'regular' at the grotty pub down the road. I'd go in at lunchtime with a couple of papers, then the other regulars would start to arrive and we'd discuss the war, Bush and Blair and, later, Dr David Kelly, Alistair Campbell, Andrew Gilligan, and the bafflingly elusive weapons of mass destruction.

But it turns out that slow suicide is not for me. I was starting to hate my reflection. My flushed, bloating face and the deadness behind the eyes. One night Ricki stopped for a quick one on the way home from lectures. We stood at the bar while she told me about Josephine's continued promiscuity, Sabrina's dropping out and her own dissertation. I tried not to slur. Then she gripped my arm, leaned in and said in my ear, "Come on, Prof. There has to be more to you than this."

"There's not," I assured her. "This is all that's left. Maybe it's all there ever was. A walking shadow."

The next day I found a flyer in my hip pocket. I had a vague memory of Ricki, giggling, shoving it in there. Had she written her number on it? No, of course she hadn't. The flyer advertised a local community centre. They wanted volunteers to work in the kitchen and run classes in 'arts and crafts'.

It turns out I can still cook, and the café is developing something of a cult following among the students. It's nice to see young faces again, and if I'm not allowed to teach them at least I can make them a decent lunch. There's a creative writing class on Monday afternoons. I make a point of not drinking Sundays, and of reading very carefully everything they write. You can see where this is going, can't you?

She's called Chantelle. She's a cleaner, mixed-race, 42, thin apart from a pleasingly full back side. She has a nervous smile and a slight stoop from days spent sweeping floors in schools and offices. I know from photographs that she used to be very pretty, but she has a badly misshapen nose that was broken by her now-imprisoned ex-husband. She listens when I talk about the Prentice case, and she seems to forgive me, more than I forgive myself. She writes poetry about beautiful things – angels whispering in rush-hour traffic, rainbows in a puddle of petrol, constellations in her coffee cup. Chantelle can't have children, and this fact sometimes wakes her up at night and makes her cry. I roll over and hold her, quivering in my arms until we sink back to sleep. She has the most lovely, smooth skin that barely seems to cover her delicate, bony shoulders. *Gently*, she whispers, when I get carried away. *Gently*. I could crush her and it scares me. Each time she tells me she loves me, and I hold her in my arms and make love to her, I endeavour to repress all that is worst in my nature, and to drag to the fore all that is pure and good. It's a day-at-a-time thing. And I'm managing so far not to hurt her.

But I do wonder about tomorrow.

And tomorrow. And tomorrow.

232